FAYE LANTERN

AND

THE SEARCH FOR THE VILLAGE MURDERER

PENNY TOWNSEND

Copyright © 2022 by Penny Townsend

All rights reserved. No part of this book may be used or reproduced by any means, graphic, electronic, or mechanical, including photocopying, recording, taping, or by any information storage retrieval system, without the written permission of the publisher except in the case of brief quotations embodied in critical articles and reviews.

AUTHOR BIO:

Penny Townsend lives in Hampshire. Her first book *Faye Lantern and the Search for the Village Murderer* - is her debut in the world of Mystery writing. As a qualified Life Coach and Counsellor, she has a unique perspective on our human qualities, which shines through in the characters she creates. It's usual to find Penny sitting in her hanging chair surrounded by colorful cushions, sipping tea from her cat mug, and trying to stop her lovable and clumsy Labrador from knocking the cup over with his tail. But most often, you'll find her at her desk, writing the next in the series of the *Fay Lantern* Mysteries.

Contents

CHAPTER ONE

Windmill Cottage

Margie couldn't stand it any longer. Seeing that smug look on Dollie's face as she sashayed past, flicking her blonde hair over her shoulder, her heels clicking on the stone path as she passed what Margie deemed tacky, clashing purple pansies and orange marigolds. Worse still, trailing behind her were Sony and Greg from their gardening club, like lost puppies, overloaded with trays of pink carnations.

"Follow me!" Dollie called out in a trill voice as they obediently followed her down the side of the old Windmill Cottage to the land at the rear of the garden. Margie ran upstairs to her bedroom window at the back of the house, which overlooked the three pristine gardens. Dollie's to the left in a riot of colors, hers in the middle in neatly matching rows of white lilies on the left and purple Veronicas on the right, and that of Mr. Pilchard, who was halfway up a ladder pruning his row of topiary birds.

Margie was sure Dollie had cheated last year at the annual Best in Bloom fair. She had turned up with the biggest prize-winning Dahlias and won best in show.

Margie hadn't seen them growing in Dollie's garden and knew someone had given them to her. Well, it wasn't going to happen this year, she had decided. She was going to wait until Dollie was out and go round into Dollie's garden to see what was growing in the far corner that was out of sight of Margie's window.

At that moment, Dollie had caught sight of Margie at the window and waved up with that smug look again, as Greg and Sony looked up to see her spying through the nets. She darted away from the window in a fluster and heard a screech as she stepped on her cat Peony's tail. Her poor Peony had been sitting silently behind her, looking out the window with her.

"Oh, Peony, I'm so sorry," she said, lifting her foot from a hissing Peony, who ran angrily out of sight. Margie picked up the pen and pad from the dressing table. She kept it there to take notes on all Dollie's activities for future reference. She wasn't being cheated out of the "Best in Bloom" title this year. She would prove to everyone that Dollie was a fraud!

CHAPTER TWO

Foul Play

It was seven thirty in the evening. Margie was pouring a glass of Juniper wine when she thought she heard raised voices coming from next door. She looked out of her window to see the downstairs light go off at Dollie's cottage. She scanned around, but everything was still and quiet. Dismissing it as nothing, she went back to preparing her script for her winning acceptance speech for this year's Best in Bloom. It was going to be hers this year—that, she was sure of.

***

Margie was awoken by a very loud banging on her front door, followed by the doorbell ringing two or three times.

"Who on earth could that be?" she muttered, still half asleep. She looked across at the clock on the bedside table and saw it was six o'clock in the morning, too early for visitors.

She sat up and swung her feet to the floor and into her neatly placed slippers. Grabbing her white dressing gown from the back of the bedroom door, she put it on and hurried down the stairs to the sound of the doorbell ringing again.

"Who is it?" she called out, seeing two large figures through the door glass.

"Police! We need a word, Mrs. Field. Open the door, please!"

Margie opened the door on the chain and peered through the gap at the two men. The taller, older of the two men stepped forward, holding out a police badge.

"Detective Inspector Rawlings. Open the door, Mrs. Field. We need to ask you a few questions."

"What about?" she asked as she opened the door fully to see the flashing blue lights of the police car outside Dollie's cottage.

"There's been a murder. We need to ask you a few routine questions. Can we come in?"

Margie noticed her hands starting to shake as she let go of the door and Inspector Rawlings and the younger policeman followed her into the living room.

Inspector Rawlings looked at Margie, staring at her intently as he spoke. "Whereabouts were you between the hours of four o'clock and midnight yesterday?"

"I was here all day yesterday and went to bed at nine o'clock," she stammered.

"Can you corroborate that?" he asked, as he walked over to where Margie's acceptance speech was lying spread out over three pages on her desk.

"No. Of course, I can't. I live on my own," she replied, watching him pick up her speech. "You said there has been a murder?"

"Take these as evidence." Inspector Rawlings gestured to the younger policeman, ignoring her question.

"Excuse me! That's my private property. I need those papers!"

"Not anymore. They are part of a murder investigation now." He turned to eye her again, as the younger officer went to search upstairs. "How well do you know Mrs. Mahoney?"

She could feel him studying the reaction on her face as she replied, "Not very well. But I do know she is a cheat and a liar." She folded her arms defiantly, thinking about the lack of prize-winning Dahlias in Dollie's garden.

She heard heavy footsteps coming back down the stairs, through the hallway, and into the living room where they were standing. The young policeman, keen to please, Margie thought, rushed forward and handed the pen and pad from her dressing table to Inspector Rawlings. There were detailed notes of Dollie's movements in and out of the cottage and precise times. On the last page, dated yesterday, Margie had written, "*Tonight is the night!*" in bold letters across the top of the page. "*She will never win again!*"

Inspector Rawlings's eyes narrowed, focusing again on Margie. "Can you explain this?" he asked, showing her the pad.

"I was going to . . . I mean, I was just . . ." She froze and fell silent, unable to explain her true intentions. She wasn't prepared to admit anything, and was even less prepared for what came next as the inspector's voice cut through the silence.

In a clear but grave tone, as he addressed her. "Mrs. Margaret Field, you are under arrest for the suspected murder of Dorothy Mahoney. You do not have to say anything, but if you do say anything, it can be used as evidence in a court of law against you. Do you understand?"

Unable to take it all in, Margie gasped. "What? You cannot be serious!"

Inspector Rawlings turned to the policeman standing next to him. "Escort Mrs. Field upstairs so she can get dressed. I'll wait for you by the car."

Margie put her hand out to steady herself on the dining room table. *This can't be happening; I'm going to wake up in a minute. This isn't real,* she thought.

"If you would, ma'am." The policeman was gesturing for her to move along upstairs to get dressed. Apart from telling the police officer that Peony had to be fed, the rest of the morning became a blur. She had no idea how she had gotten dressed or even what she was wearing. All she knew was, even in death, Dollie had ruined her day again.

CHAPTER THREE

Greg and Rosemary

Even from the kitchen, Greg could feel Rosemary's voice pierce through him as she called down from the bedroom. He made sure to cover the teapot with the cozy before he carried the tray upstairs. Rosemary's eye glanced over the tray as Greg walked in.

"I've been calling you for half an hour," she complained. Her tight blonde curls caught the sunlight coming through the curtains. Her skin was smooth and pale but still youthful, Greg thought as he leaned in to kiss her. She brushed him aside, as she always did.

"I'm not feeling well again."

Greg's face darkened for a moment as he turned away from Rosemary.

"I'm off," he said as he reached the bedroom door. "I'm going to Sony's to pick up some more plants for the display."

Rosemary looked surprised. "But you went there yesterday?"

"There's a lot of planting to do," he replied with his back to her as he walked out the door. As he made his way down the stairs, he called out, "I'll be back at teatime."

Grabbing his coat off the rack, he headed to the front door and rushed out and down the street toward Sony's house. Greg noticed the curtains were still drawn as he arrived at Sony's. Pressing the doorbell, he stepped back and watched the upstairs curtain move and fall back.

"You're early," Sony said abruptly as he opened the front door to greet him. He didn't give Greg a chance to reply before he followed it with, "I'll meet you round the back," and quickly shut the front door.

Greg reached the back gate as Sony came out of the French doors.

"The carnations are in the greenhouse. Come on."

As Greg shut the gate behind them, he heard Sony's front door slam. "Is someone inside the house with you?"

"No," Sony replied, disappearing into the greenhouse.

It didn't take them long to load the carnations into the car, and Greg followed Sony back through the French doors into the kitchen.

"I'll just grab my keys."

Greg nodded back silently, his gaze on the bright red lipstick on the rim of the coffee cup sitting on the countertop. He placed his hands around the cup—it was still warm. He caught the smell of perfume lingering in the air and bit his bottom lip, as he often did when he was irritated. It was a familiar scent.

Sony appeared in the doorway. "You ready?" he asked, looking at Greg. A puzzled look came over his face. "Your lip is bleeding!"

Greg didn't reply as he followed Sony out to the car.

It was a short trip to Dollie's cottage. The two men drove in silence until Sony said, "Look! There's Dollie," who was standing outside her cottage waving as they pulled up.

Cropped green slacks hugged her trim figure. Her long blonde hair, full and thick, fell over her shoulders and onto her short-sleeved white jumper. A bright pink scarf tied around her neck mirrored the pink of the carnations she was holding in a pot in her hands. Sony had already jumped out of the car, and opening the boot, they both loaded up the trays of pink carnations into their arms as Dolly walked over.

"Hello, boys," she said with a big smile on her face. "This way," she beckoned them as they followed her along the path that passed around the side of her cottage.

Greg shut the gate behind him with his foot and caught up with Sony and Dollie, who had both stopped and were looking up at her neighbor's window.

"Wave, boys," Dollie said with a smile. Greg noticed the curtains move and someone disappear from view, and Dollie let out a laugh. "Come along, boys. Follow me." She continued walking down the path and turned under the arch to the side of the cottage.

Greg, following behind, caught the familiar scent of perfume in the air again, and his face twisted in anger as they stopped and put down the trays of carnations.

Sony turned to Greg and handed him his car keys. "I have an engagement in town. Can you put the keys back through the letterbox when you've finished?"

He said his farewells to Dollie, and Greg noticed they seemed to linger in the embrace longer than usual. He watched Dollie, studying her every movement as she waved goodbye to Sony. They would be alone together for the whole day.

CHAPTER FOUR

The Old Station House

Roses around the door was the first thing Faye noticed when she went to view the Old Station House. "Idyllic" was the word the estate agent used to describe the house, and "lovingly converted."

"The last owner was an expert gardener," Mr. Grimmer explained, "but she became frail and had to go into a retirement home after . . ." His words trailed off as he continued further along the path. Faye couldn't disagree about the expert gardening. The path was brimming over with big, blousy white and pink hydrangeas. Their overflowing blooms felt homely and inviting leading up to an arched front door painted in mint green, with a small diamond-shaped window in the middle and surrounding the door a cascade of red roses, but it was the fireplace in the living room that really caught her attention. With a slightly gnarled oak mantelpiece, proudly sitting over a row of bricks arching over and around to frame the large open fireplace, she imagined sitting there, cozy on her sofa with the fire blazing, sketching in her art book. After seeing the light, airy room with high ceilings at the back of the house,

Faye realized the house was perfect for her and her artwork and suddenly exclaimed, “I’ll take it,” stopping Mr. Grimmer mid-sentence.

From there on in, it all happened quite quickly. With no chain, Faye found herself moving in within the month. It was a new chapter in her life, and it scared her. Nothing was familiar. Not the people, the area, or the house, and although she was way out of her comfort zone, Faye knew this was where she was meant to be.

A chink of sunlight breaking through the clouds shone through the large bay window, falling across the kitchen table as Faye now weaved her way through the wooden packing boxes. They had been unceremoniously abandoned across the kitchen and living room floor by the removal men, who had rushed off to fit in another job that afternoon. She was halfway through unpacking the box marked “kitchen” when she heard the doorbell buzz. *I must change that doorbell*, she thought, as she approached the front door.

“Just coming,” she called out, hoping it was a friendly neighbor with a welcome basket of sandwiches or pot of stew, as she had arrived at the Old Station House at eight o’clock last night and hadn’t had time to buy any groceries for her lunch today. She opened the door to see a tall figure of a man. Under a dark gray hat, his blond hair was thick and wavy and slicked down as if in an effort to control its unruliness. In stark contrast, his blue eyes seemed bright and piercing as he looked at Faye. He wore a matching charcoal-gray jacket and trousers, finished off with a checkered gray and light blue tie, which Faye noticed was leaning to one side as though pulled across. His overcoat was long and cream colored, and he had an air of authority about him as he held out his badge.

"Good afternoon, Miss Lantern," he said, tipping his hat. "I'm Detective Inspector Rawlings, Chichester Police. Petworth Police Station. I wonder if I might have a moment of your time?"

Faye was distracted by the smell of freshly baked bread as a slim woman in her mid-thirties appeared next to Inspector Rawlings holding a wicker basket. She wore a

white apron, and a blue-and-white head scarf framed her face. She beamed a huge smile as she spoke.

"Hello, I'm Gwen. I own the bakery just down the way," she said, turning her head to indicate where the bakery was. "I thought you might be in need of some lunch." Lifting the napkin from the basket, she exposed an array of sandwiches cut into small triangles, along with assorted tea cakes and biscuits.

Before Faye could respond, Gwen looked at the inspector. "Afternoon, Tom," she said, already pushing past him to walk into the hallway. "I know the way," she called out, heading toward the kitchen.

Faye opened the door wider for the inspector, who followed her into the living room. Gwen popped her head up above the kitchen worktop, followed by some side plates she had put down in a pile alongside cups she had already found in one of the packing boxes.

"That's very kind of you," Faye said, deciding to go along with Gwen's forthright approach, as she really was quite hungry. "Would you like a sandwich, Inspector?"

As he raised his hand to take a sandwich, Gwen piped up, "You'll have none left if Tom gets his hands on them!"

The inspector's hand dropped away as he glared at Gwen and back to Faye. "No, thank you, Miss Lantern. I need to speak with you in private," he said and turned back to look pointedly at Gwen, who mumbled something under her breath.

"It was nice to meet you . . ." She left a pause for Faye to fill in the gap.

"Faye."

"Pop into the bakery, Faye, if you are passing. It will be nice to have a chat and get to know you," she said as she headed to the door, smiling broadly again.

"I will." Faye nodded, then called out, "And thank you again for the sandwiches," as she watched Gwen disappear out the kitchen, leaving her alone with the inspector.

CHAPTER FIVE

Timing

"I'm afraid I must ask you this question, Miss Lantern. It's standard procedure. I need to know your whereabouts yesterday afternoon, between the hours of four o'clock and midnight."

Puzzled, Faye replied, "I arrived here last night. Just after eight o'clock. What's this about?"

"I'm sorry to say, it's not as warm a welcome as would normally be hereabouts, Miss Lantern. I'm investigating a murder."

Taken aback, Faye replied, "Oh. My goodness! Who?" before realizing it was a stupid question, as she didn't know anyone from the village.

"Dorothy Mahoney. She lived a few streets away. Can you verify what time you arrived last night?" the inspector questioned her again.

Faye scanned the kitchen, looking for her bag. Spotting it hanging over the back of the chair, she walked over and, lifting one handle off, opened it up.

"Here it is," she said, reaching in and pulling out a train ticket. She stepped around another packing box and handed the ticket to Inspector Rawlings.

"I caught the six thirty train last night and arrived at Petworth Station at seven fifty."

"May I keep this?" he asked, holding up the ticket.

Faye shrugged. "Be my guest, Inspector. I have no use for it now."

He tucked the ticket in his inside jacket pocket and reached out for a sandwich from the plate Gwen had left on the top.

Faye saw him hesitate for a second and look over to her, so she quickly nodded. "Please help yourself, Inspector. There are far too many for me to eat them all.

"Do you mind me asking," Faye continued, "how Miss Mahoney . . . erm . . . well, how she died, Inspector?"

Taking another handful of sandwiches, he said, "I'm waiting for the coroner's report, but there are signs of a struggle."

Faye noticed the inspector's voice took on a more formal tone as he continued to question her.

"Can you tell me how you got here from the train station yesterday?"

"I walked!" she replied confidently. "It takes nine minutes exactly once you leave the station."

Inspector Rawlings looked quizzically at her.

"I take notice of details," she added, answering his unspoken question.

"Well, then, Miss Lantern, perhaps you can tell me if you noticed anyone else on your nine-minute walk from the station last night? Did you notice anything you thought was suspicious or odd?"

Faye slowly moved the plate out of the inspector's reach and picked up one of the last two remaining sandwiches.

"Well, Inspector, I'm not sure if it's important, but I noticed there was a light on in the church, in the side window, and two people were talking in the doorway. The church is about halfway, so it would have been around seven fifty-five when I noticed the light."

"Could you describe the two people you saw talking in the church doorway? Were they male or female?" he asked.

Faye noticed the inspector was now focused on her every word, staring intently at her, waiting for her reply.

"Well, erm," she said awkwardly, feeling a need to get the details right. "I'm afraid it was too dark to see them clearly, it just looked like two people talking."

He started pacing back and forth, his hands clasped behind his back.

"I see. Was there anything else you noticed?" he asked, moving toward the plate again.

"No. I think that was all," she said, clutching the last sandwich in her hand as he reached for the biscuits. "I'm sorry I couldn't be more help, Inspector."

"On the contrary, Miss Lantern. You have been most helpful. I have more inquiries to follow, so I'll be off now. Thank you for the sandwiches," he said, tipping his hat. "Good day."

"Good day, Inspector," Faye replied, watching him stride quickly out through the front door. Murder, she thought. That was something she hadn't expected. She locked the front door behind him.

CHAPTER SIX

The Village Meeting

Gwen was standing outside Faye's front door talking so fast Faye missed some of the conversation.

"It starts at seven o'clock sharp tonight. We're meeting in the village hall to see if we can piece together what happened to Dollie."

Faye looked at Gwen silently, puzzled.

"Dorothy Mahoney?" Gwen added. "You know, the woman who was murdered yesterday."

Faye had been busy unpacking and had completely forgotten about the murder. "Oh! Yes, of course. I remember."

"Come along tonight, if you are not too tired," Gwen said.

"I'm not sure I will be of any help," Faye replied. "I didn't arrive until late yesterday." She hoped that would be sufficient enough an excuse to get her out of attending the meeting.

Unfazed, Gwen replied, "Maybe I'll see you later, then?"

"Maybe," Faye answered.

That seemed to suffice, as Gwen said, "Great! Don't forget. It starts at seven thirty," and rushed off.

Faye had decided not to go to the meeting when the doorbell buzzed later that night. She opened the door to see Gwen standing there in a scarlet-red jacket and matching hat sitting on top of her blonde, neatly bobbed hair.

"Me again." She smiled. "Can you come to the hall to settle something, Faye, about the light you saw at the church? Tom . . . Inspector Rawlings asked me to fetch you, he's there now," she added quickly, noticing Faye's look of hesitance about going with her.

Faye put on her navy swing coat and reluctantly headed off with Gwen on the short walk to the village hall. She could hear Inspector Rawlings's voice booming out as they arrived: "Sony, calm down."

Faye could feel all eyes turn upon her as she walked in with Gwen, and as interest turned to the newcomer in their midst, the hall fell silent.

"This is Miss Lantern," Gwen announced. "She is the new owner of the Old Station House."

There was a murmur in the crowd, a few heads acknowledging her, nodding at her as she walked with

Gwen to the front, where Inspector Rawlings was standing.

"Thank you for coming, Miss Lantern. This is not an official meeting, you understand. I've come along to make sure the peace is kept, nothing more," he said.

As the inspector spoke, Faye noticed a small, slightly balding man sitting in the front row. He had a neat, tidy appearance, wearing a black suit with a stiff, narrow white collar, which Faye recognized instantly as the collar worn by the vicar.

"Can you tell the vicar what you saw last night, please, Miss Lantern?" the inspector continued, gesturing toward him.

Faye started to feel uncomfortable. The vicar was staring at her, his eyes boring into her.

"Well . . . erm . . . well. I saw a light on at the side of the church, and two figures in the entrance," she said, straightening up, trying to overcome her unease at his constant glower upon her.

"You are mistaken, Miss Lantern," the vicar interrupted. "You must have seen a reflection of the streetlamp; sometimes it plays tricks on your eyes in the dark."

"No. It was definitely a light I saw," she repeated, but the Vicar was adamant.

"It's not possible!" he retorted, turning to face Inspector Rawlings. "I have the only set of keys to the front door of the church. I locked up last night. There were no break-ins, as the alarm would have gone off if anyone was there."

He turned again to face Faye. "I'm sorry, Miss Lantern, but I'm afraid you are mistaken."

As the vicar rose from his seat, Faye suddenly let out a gasp, making the vicar turn to look at her. "I remember something from last night!"

"Oh!" Inspector Rawlings said with interest.

"Yes. I remember hearing the clicking of heels on the pavement, women's heels," she added, "like the sound stiletto heels make."

"Well, this has nothing to do with the church!" the vicar blurted out. "Two people in the dark, a noise that sounds like stiletto heels. It's all very vague, Miss Lantern. I imagine you were very tired by that time of night after moving house, and it's easy to imagine things in the dark when you are tired, especially," he exaggerated, "when you are not a local and unfamiliar with your surroundings."

Faye stood dumbfounded, unable to reply, as the vicar was already walking quickly through the middle of the hall toward the exit in somewhat of a rush, desperate to get away as people started to get up from their seats.

Faye watched him leave the hall and then turned to Inspector Rawlings.

"I am very clear that my account is accurate, Inspector Rawlings." Faye paused before adding, "I think the vicar knows more than he is letting on."

CHAPTER SEVEN

Daniel and Buster

Faye liked to walk. She needed some fresh air and a break from the unpacking and was just about to leave, when she heard a car pull up outside. Opening the front door, she saw Buster, her two-year-old Golden Labrador, jump out of the taxi, followed by the desperate call of Daniel, her nephew, being dragged out of the car, just managing to hold on to the door to save himself from being pulled over as Buster charged across the path and spun in circles, wagging his tail at the sight of Faye.

"You're here! I'm so pleased to see you both," she said, making a fuss over Buster. "How was your trip?"

"Fabulous! We saw some lovely sights, and Buster was sick in the car!"

Daniel looked at the footwell in the rear of the car just as the driver got out and started to complain. Faye immediately apologized, offering to pay for the car to be cleaned and for any inconvenience caused.

"You must be exhausted!" she said after, ushering them inside. "It's so good to see you!" She kissed Daniel lightly on both cheeks.

Buster had already found his favorite chair with his cushion on it and made himself comfortable as Faye moved boxes to clear a path to the table.

"How did Frank take the news?" she called out to Daniel as he carried his suitcase in.

"Not well. He said he had lost one of the most promising young accountants he had seen in a while."

Faye stopped and turned to look at Daniel. With concern in her voice, she said, "If you change your mind and want to go back, it's okay. I'm fine here. You don't have to worry about me."

"No," he said, trying to sound convincing, "I've made my decision to leave and come here, for better or worse. I'll live with the consequences."

Faye, half-smiling, looked around at the chaos. Surrounded by boxes and furniture all in the wrong place.

"It's new for both of us. It's a big change, and I'm nervous too, but we have each other to lean on, and that is a blessing," she said, patting his arm. "Now, let's get you to your apartment upstairs."

The Station House was divided into two. There was a separate staircase at the front of the house leading upstairs to a self-contained apartment. Daniel made his way upstairs and looked around at the spacious but dusty and tired apartment. Putting both hands on his hips, he sighed, hoping he had made the right choice, as it was too late to change back now.

CHAPTER EIGHT

The Vicarage

Faye had awoken early to the sound of Buster barking. She could tell by his bark that he was trying to get her attention. If somebody had been there, his bark would have deepened, but as Faye walked into the kitchen, Buster was waiting by the door, eager to go out into the garden.

It was around seven o'clock, and by eight thirty, Faye was putting on Buster's lead and heading down the road and through the fields that led to the old bridge behind the vicarage. The air was crisp as she walked into the vicarage grounds, and she noticed the headstones, aged with gray lichen, seemed to look peaceful as the morning sun danced around them, every now and then glancing its light across the buttercups and daises sprinkled through the grass. She stopped to read a few of the names on the headstones. That's odd, she thought. At that moment, Buster barked, and turning the corner, Inspector Rawlings came striding into view. Approaching her, he tipped his hat, with one eye on Buster, who was grumbling under his breath.

"I'm so sorry, Inspector. He doesn't like hats."

Inspector Rawlings slowly took off his hat and held it in one hand down by his side. Buster immediately transformed and started wagging his tail.

"He's a rescue dog, and I think something about hats seems to upset him," she said apologetically.

"I see. No harm done," he said, and patted Buster on the head.

"May I ask, are you on police business, Inspector?" she said, looking over at the vicarage.

The inspector stopped petting Buster and gave him a biscuit from his pocket before turning to Faye.

"I was waiting to speak with the vicar, but he isn't answering the door."

Faye looked around. "Is there a side door?"

"I was just on my way there."

Faye followed Inspector Rawlings around the vicarage to the back of the church to see an arched door standing half-open.

"That's strange," he said, walking in, followed by Faye and Buster.

As Inspector Rawlings called out for the vicar, Buster took off and started to drag Faye down through the middle of the church.

"Buster! Stop!" she said, pulling him back on his lead, but Buster didn't stop until he reached the vestry door at the side of the altar, where he stood barking.

Inspector Rawlings was a step behind Faye when she let out a terrified scream as she opened the vestry door. There, sprawled across the floor in a blood-soaked cassock, was the vicar.

Faye heard the sound of approaching sirens as she sat on the wooden bench outside the vicarage, with Buster lying at her feet. She could see Inspector Rawlings talking with several officers, before he turned and headed over in her direction.

He was careful to take off his hat as he neared Faye and Buster, who was sitting like a lion on guard at Faye's feet, as though sensing her distress.

"That was quite a shock, Miss Lantern," he said as he reached Faye.

She shook her head from side to side whilst pursing her lips, which she always did when she was deep in thought.

"Why would anyone want to . . ." She stopped for a moment, then shook her head. "It doesn't make any sense."

"Crimes are often senseless," Inspector Rawlings replied.

"Well, I think there is more to it." Faye stood up from her seat, making Buster jump up, ready to spring into action. Faye was still thinking about the crime scene she had just witnessed. "I noticed there was a candlestick lying on the floor, a brass one, in the blood."

"That would probably be the murder weapon," Inspector Rawlings said.

"But why would the murderer leave it behind?" Faye questioned, looking at the inspector.

"The murderer probably panicked or got disturbed," he answered, then added, "It's being sent to the lab now to see if the murderer left any prints on it. We've spoken to everyone the vicar was in contact with this morning; there aren't any witnesses at the moment."

"That may not be entirely accurate, Inspector."

"Oh?" he replied. Looking surprised at Faye.

"I believe there is a witness here." Faye put out her arm in a wide sweep of the graveyard. "Even the dead can tell secrets."

Inspector Rawlings scratched his head, wondering if the shock had had more effect on Faye than he realized. Before he could say anything else, Faye started walking toward a headstone at the entrance of the graveyard.

"Over here!" she called, beckoning the inspector to her. "When I came here earlier on my walk, I stopped to read some of the names on the headstones. I always wonder who they were and what their lives were like. This headstone here," she said, pointing to a white angel standing on top of a square marble block that made up the headstone, "I was reading the name 'William.'" She pointed to the engraved letters.

"I can't see how this is helping," the inspector interrupted.

"Just look closer," Faye said, urging him to bend down so his eyes would be in line with the words.

Sighing, he moved forward. "I don't think . . ." His words stopped abruptly as Faye moved some ivy that had trailed down, slightly covering the words, to reveal a clear red handprint just to the side of the angel.

"Well, well, well," he said, looking back at Faye. "That is interesting!"

"I couldn't work out what it was at first," she explained. "But now . . . after seeing the vicar's body . . ."

"Quite," Inspector Rawlings said to Faye's unspoken words. He called out to one of the police constables standing nearby and asked him to stand guard until they could get the police photographer over.

"The murderer may have tripped and put their hand out," she added, walking around the headstone. "I can't see why else there would be a bloodstained handprint here."

Puzzled, Inspector Rawlings watched as Faye suddenly stopped and bent down by the headstone. Picking up a single leaf, she held it up to show the inspector.

"Do you see?" She pointed to a small circle in the leaf.

Inspector Rawlings took the leaf from Faye and turning it over, he murmured, "The type of indentation a stiletto heel would make." Sighing, he added, "I'm afraid this has just made things a lot more complicated."

Faye stood up again to speak to the inspector. "Two deaths in two days, Inspector. I believe they may be linked. I want to check on something this afternoon, Inspector. I have a hunch."

"I don't believe in hunches, Miss Lantern," he replied, pulling a white handkerchief out of his pocket, and after carefully wrapping the leaf in it added, "Cold hard facts are what we need."

"Oh, they'll turn up, Inspector, I'm sure."

Until then, she thought as she bid goodbye to the inspector, *I will need to do a bit more digging.* Faye walked out of the churchyard, her mind set on visiting a certain someone on the street who, she was positive, knew more than they were letting on.

CHAPTER NINE

Mrs. Field

Being arrested in broad daylight was as bad as it could get for Margie, who was sitting down on the cell bed, her foot tapping quickly. She suddenly jumped up and started banging on the cell door. After getting over the shock of being arrested, she came to realize she was in a very serious situation.

"I demand to speak with Detective Inspector Rawlings!" she said, raising her voice and continuing to bang on the cell door. "I have been falsely arrested!"

She heard the rattle of keys approaching her cell, and with each hand clasped by her side and teeth clenched, prepared herself to engage with Detective Inspector Rawlings. She was going to demand to be allowed a telephone call to her lawyer to sort this fiasco out.

As the cell door opened, a woman she didn't recognize stood there. Margie guessed she was in her thirties. She was smartly dressed in a blue swing coat, and her green eyes stood out, framed by shoulder-length auburn hair, as she spoke.

"Hello, Mrs. Field. I'm Faye Lantern, and I was wondering whether I could speak with you for a moment?"

Margie looked past Faye, her eyes searching for the inspector.

"Where is Detective Inspector Rawlings?" she asked, looking back at Faye.

"He's not here at the moment. He's at the vicarage. Unfortunately, there's been another murder. The vicar, to be precise."

Margie took a step back, and Faye caught her arm to steady her, helping her to sit back down on the cell bed.

"Constable, could you please fetch Mrs. Field a glass of water?"

Margie noticed the uncertainty in his eyes at leaving Faye with her unattended.

"We will be just fine here."

His eyes shifted between the two of them sitting on the cell bed before locking the door behind him and walking away.

Faye turned to Margie. "I was at the vicarage today, Mrs. Field, and I was the one who discovered the vicar's body. I think his and Dorothy Mahoney's murders may be linked."

Margie's eyes narrowed. "That woman is still the bane of my life, even after her—" Margie stopped mid-sentence, dismissing what she'd been planning to say next. "Well, you know what I mean," she said, looking at Faye.

Faye nodded. "Mrs. Field, do you mind me asking if you have any idea why Inspector Rawlings has charged you with the suspected murder of Dorothy Mahoney?"

Margie threw her hands in the air. "Of course, not! It's a huge mistake and he is a complete fool! I've been locked up in here since yesterday morning. I haven't been interviewed by him or even been able to speak with my lawyer!" She stopped and froze, before breaking down in tears. "I want to go home," she sobbed. "Peony will be missing me, wondering where her dinner is."

"Peony?" Faye asked, handing Margie a tissue from her bag.

"My cat," she replied, sniffing. "You're new here. Are you on holiday?" she asked, staring at Faye.

Faye shook her head. "No. I've just moved into the Old Station House."

"The old tearooms, you mean. Mrs. Penny used to run it before she went into the retirement home last year."

Faye nodded in agreement, trying to conceal her surprise. The estate agent hadn't mentioned any of that to her, but she wanted to keep Mrs. Field focused, as she knew she didn't have long before Inspector Rawlings would be back, and she might not get another opportunity.

"Mrs. Field," she began again, "how well did you know Mrs. Mahoney?"

"She was my neighbor. I knew of her comings and goings, but that was all," she replied defensively. The sharp contours of her face were just visible against the dim lighting as she continued. "I didn't much care for her, truth be told." She became agitated. "But I didn't murder her. Not for the cup! I had other means for her to be found out as a liar and a cheat!"

"The cup?" Faye inquired.

"For Best in Bloom! She has won it three years in a row, and last year, she won with Dahlias, and she didn't grow a single Dahlia! Not a one! Which, by the way, is in the rules, you must grow your own. So how did she win?"

Faye shrugged.

"Well, let's just say she knew the flower show judges very well. More than well!"

"I see." Faye nodded.

"She seemed to have some magic power when it came to men. Those boys followed her around like puppies."

"Which boys?" Faye asked, urging her to continue.

"Sony and Greg. They were there two days ago, on Wednesday, with her, carrying trays of plants into her garden."

"Can you remember what time that was?"

"It was about nine o'clock in the morning. That's when I saw them, before Dollie's . . ." Her voice cut short. "It's all written in my diary, which Detective Inspector Rawlings has," she added, getting irritated again.

"I'm sorry to keep asking you, Mrs. Field, but did you notice what time they left?"

"Sony left soon after, but I saw Greg in the garden in the afternoon. It was around four o'clock when he left. I noticed the back gate was open again at seven thirty, that's when I heard voices."

"What's going on here?" Inspector Rawlings asked, walking in with the officer who had gone to fetch the glass of water.

"I was just speaking with Mrs. Field," Faye replied in a fluster and jumped up, swiftly followed by Mrs. Field, who added, “Inspector Rawlings, I demand you release me at once!”

“We have a few questions to ask you, Mrs. Field, then we will review the situation.”

Faye saw her chance to escape and side-stepped Inspector Rawlings, quickly walking out the door as Margie started arguing with him again.

CHAPTER TEN

The "Flower Show" Cup

Faye couldn't contain her excitement, pulling the square package from one of the wooden packing boxes as Daniel appeared in the doorway.

"You sound like you've found something exciting! Is that toast I smell?" he said and wandered into the kitchen.

"It's my chessboard," she said, opening the brown paper wrapping to reveal a worn but ornately carved wooden box. "I used to spend hours as a child playing chess with my father."

"I remember Dad and Uncle Colin playing." He smiled. "Back in the day."

Faye loved her father dearly and knew the one game he had loved to play was chess. Seeing her opportunity to spend time with him as a child, she'd persuaded him to teach her how to play, and sometimes one game would take several days.

"You can't rush a move, you have to plan and strategize," her father used to say.

So, Faye had gotten every book she could find on chess from the library. It was there she'd met Tommy. He had been studying for his exams and happened to notice that Faye was avidly reading every chess book in the library, and then one day, he'd brought in his chessboard for them to play on. Faye had managed to become quite a good player and when war broke out a few years later, Tommy left the board with Faye to look after for him in memory of their time together. Faye had written regularly to him when he went to war, until she received a message from his family letting her know he was missing in action. Now, the board was the only memory she had of Tommy and the chess games she'd shared with him and with her father, who had recently passed away.

"Do you play?" she asked, looking over at Daniel, who was pulling spoonfuls of jam out of the jar and spreading them onto his toast.

"Me! Oh, no. I can't play for toffee. I tried once. I played for a bet in the local pub, and it was awful. I warned him I'd never played before, but he wouldn't listen."

"You lost the bet, then?" Faye asked.

"No. I won! Of course, I told him it was just beginner's luck, but he insisted I play him again, and after I beat him two more times, he was so angry he smashed the table up!"

"Oh, dear!" Faye said. She was just about to convince Daniel to let her teach him when there was a knock at the door.

Daniel put his toast back down on the plate. "I'll get it."

A few moments later, he returned, followed by Inspector Rawlings, hat in hand and out of view of Buster, who had followed Daniel to the front door and back and was now investigating the contents of the packing box Faye had just opened.

"Inspector Rawlings. I wasn't expecting to see you so soon!" Faye greeted him sheepishly, remembering her swift exit from Margie's cell earlier that day.

"Well, Miss Lantern, although we both discovered the vicar . . . the murder victim together, I didn't ask you where you were between the hours of midnight last night and ten o'clock this morning. It's procedure, you understand. I have to ask," he added, shifting uncomfortably from one foot to the other.

"I understand, Inspector," Faye replied, setting up the last player on the chessboard. She looked back at the inspector. "I was here all evening."

"Can anyone else corroborate that?" he asked, looking over at Daniel.

"Sorry, I was down at the pub with John from Barnham Solicitors. They want me to do some accounting for them."

"Oh, that is good news, Daniel," Faye replied.

"Yes, I'm quite chuffed with myself at getting hired the first day I've been here."

"Congratulations, Daniel," Inspector Rawlings interjected, "but can we please get back to the question, Miss Lantern?"

Faye thought about the previous night of the seventeenth. "I telephoned my sister around eight thirty and I finished the call about nine fifteen."

Inspector Rawlings raised his eyebrows in surprise.

"We had a lot to catch up on!" she added quickly.

Inspector Rawlings paced back and forth, something Faye noticed he did quite frequently when he was thinking.

"Well, I'll leave you both to it, I don't want to be late for my first day," Daniel said, heading out of the room and leaving Faye and Inspector Rawlings together.

"I'm sorry I couldn't be more help, Inspector," Faye continued. "But I was tucked up in bed from ten o'clock that night and," she added before he could ask her another question, "I only have Buster as a witness."

The inspector stopped pacing as Faye finished speaking.

"If you wouldn't mind making a statement down at the station to confirm what you have just told me, along with your account of yesterday's events at the vicarage, I would appreciate it. It will also corroborate my account of the event."

"I'll pop by later today." She smiled. "Do you play?" she asked, her hand gesturing toward the chessboard.

Inspector Rawlings walked over to the chessboard and moved a knight. "I was school champion!"

Faye's face lit up. She moved her own knight forward, excited that the game was on.

"Inspector Rawlings, when I spoke to Mrs. Field yesterday, she inferred that Dollie, Mrs. Mahoney, was somehow cheating in the flower show to win the Best in Bloom gold cup again. That she managed to manipulate the judges somehow each year."

Moving his knight again, the inspector shook his head. "I doubt she would have managed that this year. The vicar was the judge, and he was very strict about . . ." He stopped mid-sentence.

"The vicar was the flower show judge?" she repeated.

"If you don't mind, Miss Lantern, maybe we could finish this game another time. I have someone I need to speak with urgently."

"Of course!" Faye replied, watching him turn so fast his coat flapped up behind him as he rushed out the door.

CHAPTER ELEVEN

Unanswered Questions

Later that day after the inspector's visit, Faye took a short walk down through the village.

Gwen saw Faye and came rushing out of the bakery. "I heard about the vicar," she said, throwing her arms around Faye in a bear hug. "How awful for you, discovering him like that! It must have been such a shock!"

Taken aback, Faye had to wait for Gwen's arms to loosen their hold before she could catch her breath to reply. "I'm quite okay and over the shock now but thank you."

Stepping back, she smiled at Gwen, who always seemed to be covered in flour. "I'm just off to the station now, to fill in a statement."

"I won't keep you, then. Maybe you could call in sometime for a cup of tea when you are passing?"

"That would be lovely, Gwen," Faye said, stepping back again to avoid another hug. "I will," she added and continued her walk to the station.

***

"Ah, Miss Lantern." Inspector Rawlings appeared on the step behind Faye. She was just leaving the station after filling in her statement. "I'm on my way to Sony Baldwin's house. Are you walking that way?"

Smiling, she replied, "I'm going back through the village again, if that's where he lives?"

"My apologies, Miss Lantern. I forgot you are new here. Yes, he lives on the edge of the village, a few streets down from where Mrs. Mahoney's cottage is."

"He was there on the day of her murder, I believe," Faye replied.

"You know about him?" he asked, surprised.

"Mrs. Field," Faye answered, seeing the questioning look on his face. "She mentioned it to me the other day," she added, quickening her step to keep up with him. "She told me Sony and Greg were both at Mrs. Mahoney's that day."

The inspector nodded. "She told us that, too. Some of my officers are on their way to question Greg . . . Mr. Bulmer now."

Faye continued walking as the inspector stopped at Sony's house. Rounding the bend, she was nearly bowled over by a man rushing out of his front gate. Before she could catch her breath, a smartly dressed woman appeared at the front door. She wore a dark brown coat and had tight blond curls. Rushing past Faye, she called out, "Greg! Stop!" and continued running as fast as she could in her high-heeled black stilettoes. Faye stood for a moment, then turned back toward the station. Inspector Rawlings was still out, and she left a message for him to contact her and then set out for home again.

Buster was waiting for Faye when she arrived back at the Station House. He had discovered his lead, which Faye had placed on the table in the hallway, and was wagging his tail expectantly, with the lead dangling from his mouth.

Faye laughed. How could she resist those big, brown puppy eyes, which Buster seemed to have perfected, looking back at her, especially at walk time or dinner time?

Faye enjoyed a short walk with Buster and arrived back just in time to hear the telephone ringing.

"Miss Lantern," came the reply. "It's Inspector Rawlings. You left a message saying you needed to speak with me?"

"Thank you, Inspector, for calling me. I wanted to let you know that on my way back today, a man called Greg nearly knocked me over."

"I'm sorry to hear that, Miss Lantern," Inspector Rawlings replied.

"Oh, I'm not worried about that, Inspector," Faye said. "It was the woman who came out of the house behind him. She was wearing stiletto heels, and it just got me thinking about the mark on the leaves at the gravestone."

"What did she look like?" he asked.

"She had curly blonde hair, slim build, and was wearing a caramel-colored coat."

"That sounds like Greg's wife," he said.

"Yes, she called out 'Greg' as she ran after him down the street. I just wondered whether you might find mud on her heels that matches the earth at the gravestone?"

"I may well do," he agreed. "Rosemary, Greg's wife, is the cleaner at the vicarage, so she would have to walk through the graveyard to get to work."

"I see. That is interesting," she replied.

"Well, thank you for the information, Miss Lantern. We are looking for them both now. Once we have spoken with them, we may have a better idea of the events. Have a good day," he said, and Faye knew he was in a rush as always to get on.

"You too, Inspector." She put the receiver down.

Faye couldn't settle that night. She knew that there was something forming in her mind, like a chess game, where you place all the pieces out in your mind before you move, to see how it will play out with your opponent. Only, she was still figuring out what the next move was.

CHAPTER TWELVE

George

It was seven o'clock in the morning when Faye heard the telephone ringing. She managed to get out of bed and walk to the top of the landing when she heard Daniel's voice answering the telephone.

"I'll get her now, please hold the line."

Daniel appeared at the bottom of the stairs.

"Auntie Faye," he called up. "It's for you. A Mrs. Field?"

As Faye reached the telephone, she acknowledged Daniel, who was gesturing with Buster's lead that he was going to take Buster for a walk. As a rule, he didn't like dogs, but Buster had managed to win him over, as he usually did to get what he wanted.

"Hello, Mrs. Field?" Faye inquired.

"Yes. Hello, Faye. I just thought you might want to know that someone is in Dollie's garden. I can hear them moving around and I heard a crash, as though a pot had fallen on the floor and smashed. I just thought, as you were interested the other day."

"Thank you for letting me know, Mrs. Field. I'm glad the inspector had the good sense to let you go home," Faye said softly. "Are you sure it's a person in Dollie's garden?" she continued. "And not a cat or a fox knocking things over?"

"No! It's not!" Margie replied without hesitation. "I looked out of my window and saw the gate being shut. It has a latch you can lift from the inside to close the gate."

"That's most helpful . . . and observant of you, Mrs. Field. I'll let the inspector know." And with that, she said her goodbyes.

It only took a few minutes for the police cars to pull up and several officers to descend on Dollie's garden through the side gate.

***

"We didn't find anyone at Mrs. Mahoney's," Inspector Rawlings said, opening his wallet at the bakery to pay Gwen for his Belgian bun, later that day. Faye had already purchased her loaf and started walking out with the inspector.

"Do you have any idea who it might have been or why they were there?"

"Not yet, but forensics are at the scene now. We found a footprint. Looks like a man's boot, approximately size nine. We are cross-referencing it to see if it's a match with anything we have on record."

"You have some clues now, Inspector," Faye said, smiling, whilst trying to keep up with the inspector's quickening pace.

"Not clues. Evidence, Miss Lantern," he mumbled, taking a bite of his bun still in the bag.

Faye and the inspector parted ways at the end of the road, the inspector heading toward the station and Faye turning the corner to head back home. More boxes to unpack fleeted through her mind and she decided to take a detour first and walked down by the canal and found a bench by the water. The ducks were looking expectantly at her, and she didn't have the heart not to share a little of the loaf she had in her basket with them.

"Too much bread isn't good for them . . . so I've heard," a voice called out.

Faye turned to see a gray-haired man, well-dressed in a beige suit, lifting his hat as he approached her.

"May I?" he asked, looking at the empty seat on the bench next to Faye.

Faye nodded.

"Grain is the best thing to feed them," he added, throwing out a handful as several ducks came flapping and rushing out of the water to land at his feet.

He held out his bag of grain for Faye to take some. "I haven't seen you around here before."

Taking a small handful and throwing it to the ducks still in the water, she replied, "Thank you. I've just moved here . . . into the Old Station House."

"Ah, Penny's old place. I know it well," he replied.

"You're a local, then?"

"Born and bred. Worked on the canals my whole life. Now, I spend my days walking and feeding the ducks rather than working. But I'm happy," he said with a smile. He held out his hand. "I'm George!"

"Faye," she replied, shaking his hand.

He nodded and settled back before speaking again. "I come here to enjoy the peace and tranquility." At that moment, the ducks broke into a loud squabble, quacking and flying up, flapping their wings and arguing over the food, and she turned to look at George. They both laughed out loud.

"I'm here avoiding packing boxes." She smiled, and looking around at the green fields and trees flanked by the canal, which had several barges moored along the riverbank, she added, "It is very lovely here."

"It's a good place for thinking," he said, and Faye noticed he seemed to become distant, lost in his own thoughts for a moment.

She sat in the shared silence between them and felt the most peaceful she had since arriving.

"Unfortunately, I can't avoid those packing boxes any longer," she said, breaking the silence. She got up to leave. "Thank you for sharing the grain," she added as he tipped his hat again.

It had been an enjoyable encounter, meeting George, and she hoped their paths would cross again someday, as she left the canal to walk the short distance back home.

Faye was met by Daniel and Inspector Rawlings as she reached the Station House.

"There you are." Daniel smiled. "I was about to go looking for you."

"I just stopped to feed the ducks by the canal," Faye said, puzzled.

"Well, I'm glad you're here now," Inspector Rawlings said, opening the door of the police car. "I need you to come with me!"

"I'm not in trouble, am I?" she asked him hesitantly.

"Nothing of the sort. It's just some evidence I need to be sure about."

Relieved, Faye said goodbye to Daniel and Buster, who had managed to sneak out the front door and was sniffing out the freshly baked loaf Faye had given Daniel, which was tucked under his arm.

It wasn't long before they arrived at the vicarage.

"I would like you to help me with something, Miss Lantern—at the crime scene. Are you able to do that, or would it be too upsetting for you?" he asked softly.

"I'm quite over the shock, Inspector, and I'm happy to assist."

Inspector Rawlings nodded, and Faye followed him into the vestry where the vicar's dead body had been lying on the floor. The blood had dried into a dark patch where the vicar's head had lain, and Faye felt her stomach turn. Noticing the color drain from her face, Inspector Rawlings placed his hand under her arm to steady her.

"You don't have to do this, if it's too distressing."

Faye waved him away. "No. I'll be fine." Taking a deep breath in and out, she asked, "What do you want me to do?

"I would like you to imagine the vicar is lying bleeding on the floor, and I want you to walk over to him. You care about him and want to help him."

Faye looked at the inspector for a moment, then turned and walked toward the imaginary dead body, careful to step around the blood-stained outline on the floor. She went to the right-hand side of where the vicar's head would have been and knelt down.

"Good," the inspector said. "Now, if you would, Miss Lantern, stand up to leave."

Faye put her right hand down on the floor as she started to get back up.

"That's what I thought!"

Faye looked at him with a puzzled expression. "What do you mean?" she asked, straightening up and brushing her hands together to remove any particles of dust.

"We found fingerprints on the floor next to the vicar's body, here." He pointed to the area just above the vicar's head. Close to where Faye had just put her hand as she stood up.

"Oh!" Faye said in surprise.

"I couldn't work out why they were there," the inspector continued. "You have just shown me that if you knelt down by the body and then stood up again, the fingerprints would be on the right-hand side. We also found blood smeared across the vicar's face, as though it had been wiped off."

Faye thought for a moment. "If it was someone I cared for, I would have held them in my arms. Maybe held their head and wiped the blood away."

"Exactly, Miss Lantern, and when you put the body down again, you would have put your hands back down here." He pointed to the floor where the vicar's head had been. "Just as you demonstrated earlier."

Faye nodded. "So, the handprint would have been facing a little inward, towards the vicar's body."

"Yes," the inspector agreed, rocking back and forth from his heels to his toes as he spoke.

"Do you have any idea who the murderer is?" she asked, still uncertain as to what the inspector was heading toward.

"At this stage, it's not certain, but the fingerprints we found on the floor match the fingerprints on the gravestone." He paused and then added, "I believe we are looking at a female being the main suspect, as the handprint was too small to belong to a man."

Faye could feel the pieces starting to fit together. "So, a female, who was here, and was wearing stiletto heels." Pausing for a moment to think, she added, "Didn't you say Greg's wife Rosemary worked here as a cleaner? So, she would have access to the vicarage."

Faye's mind flashed back to the scene in the street where she was nearly knocked over by Greg, followed by Rosemary, who had come out after him wearing stiletto heels. The inspector had come to the same conclusion and was calling in on his radio to bring Rosemary into the station for fingerprinting.

"Well, Miss Lantern, you have been of great assistance this morning," the inspector said as they pulled up outside the Station House.

"Thank you, Inspector. Would you like to come in for a cup of tea?"

"It's nearly lunch time," he said, checking his watch. "I have a few minutes."

And after locking the car, he followed Faye inside.

With a brisk step, he headed straight over to the chessboard. "It's my move, I believe," he called out as Faye put the kettle on.

A few minutes later, Faye set down a tray of tea and scones and looked across at the chessboard. "That's an interesting move," she said, studying the board.

Inspector Rawlings moved back and forth, bobbing forward slightly on his toes as he loaded his plate with scones. Buster sat, looking intently at Inspector Rawlings, edging closer and closer to him, until the inspector folded and asked Faye, "Can Buster have some?" He held up a piece of scone from his plate.

"Just a small piece," she said.

Inspector Rawlings shared his scone with Buster whilst Faye moved her piece. The inspector was on his second move when the telephone rang.

"It's for you, Inspector," Faye said, holding up the telephone.

Inspector Rawlings spoke abruptly into the receiver. "I see. Thank you. I'm on my way." He hung up and turned to Faye. "My men have Rosemary in custody; I need to get back to the station. Thank you for the tea and scones, Miss Lantern."

Buster was lying quite deliberately across the front door, lying on his back with all four paws in the air, barring the way and forcing Inspector Rawlings stop in his tracks.

Thinking for a moment, he turned to Faye. "Would it be okay to give Buster some more of the scone?" He looked sheepishly at Faye, who nodded in agreement. Pulling out a scone he had wrapped earlier from his pocket, he held it out. Buster jumped up and walked over to the inspector, sniffing the air, tail wagging.

"I could have moved him," Faye said, feeling slightly embarrassed that Buster seemed to have held the inspector to ransom for another piece of scone.

"No, no," he replied. "Buster and I have reached an agreement," he said happily, petting Buster on the head as he strode out the door.

CHAPTER THIRTEEN

Beyond Reasonable Doubt

It wasn't long before Faye realized she had left her silk scarf at the vicarage. She had taken it off, fearing it would drape on the blood-stained floor when she knelt down. She pondered if someone would be there to answer the door for a moment, before deciding it was only a short distance to walk and she would take a chance.

"I'm just going over to the vicarage, Daniel," she called out, but he hadn't heard her. He was busy moving his packing boxes, which had arrived that morning, to the shed for safe keeping until he had time to deal with them. Faye left a note to say where she was going and left for the vicarage.

There was a chill in the air as she stepped outside. She pulled her coat tightly around herself and headed off. She was surprised to see the door to the vicarage was open when she arrived.

"Hello, is anybody there?" she called out. After calling out again without success, Faye stepped inside and headed to the vestry, where she found her scarf on the chair, next to the crime scene. She grabbed it quickly and was about to leave when a man's voice startled her.

"Hello, Faye. We meet again!"

She turned to see George standing there smiling at her. His eyes were sunken and his face tired, as though he hadn't slept in a while. He ran a hand through his white hair, which although disheveled in appearance, highlighted his tanned face, giving him a sort of rugged handsomeness.

"George!" she said, surprised to see him. "What are you doing here?"

"I'm just clearing out my brother's things." He stood, holding a box full of photographs, old sermons written on paper, and a few torn, shabby books that had seen better days stood half upright, next to a small silver cross, its chain hanging down over the side of the box.

"He wasn't big on material things," he said, pausing to look down at the contents of the box, "but I wanted to get on with it." His voice changed, sounded more upbeat.

"You're the vicar's brother!" Faye said, unable to hide the surprise in her voice.

"Older brother, to be exact."

"I'm so sorry for your loss. I didn't realize you were his brother."

George shrugged. "Thank you, but we weren't that close. He was a hypocrite, truth be told, and I never liked that side of him."

"A hypocrite, what do you mean?" Faye asked softly, noticing the strain on his face as he spoke.

"I know you shouldn't talk ill of the dead, but I think his double standards may have had a hand in his death."

Faye watched in silence as he bent down, carefully placing the box he had been holding onto the edge of the rectangle-shaped red carpet that ran around the main wooden floor.

Straightening up, he added. "I came to one of his sermons and listened to him preach about sin and being honest and faithful, but he wasn't able to live by those standards himself."

He flicked through a small, tattered hymn book he was still holding in his hand and stopped at one of the pages that was folded over to mark its place.

"This was his favorite hymn at Christmas. 'O, Come All Ye Faithful.' But he wasn't," he said with a look of sadness in his eyes.

"How so?" Faye asked, just as a note fell from the hymn book.

He reached down and picked it up. "'Can't wait until tonight. M.,'" he said, reading the note aloud.

At that moment, a burly removal man in cream-colored overalls and a brown cap came in, dabbing the sweat from his brow with a handkerchief.

"Is the leather chair by the vicar's desk going, gov?"

"Yes. I'll be out in a moment," George replied, agitated.

"May I?" she asked, holding her hand out toward the note.

George held out the square piece of paper for Faye to take.

"Who is 'M.,' I wonder?" Faye said aloud as she read the note, then turned it over to look at the back, which was disappointingly blank.

George shook his head. "I've no idea."

"Would you mind if I keep this?" Faye asked, holding the note up. "I would like Inspector Rawlings to take a look."

He nodded and then held out the hymn book.

"You may as well give him this, too, as the note was in it." He shrugged. "It may hold some more clues." He paused for a moment. "Although we had our differences, Roger . . . the vicar, wasn't a bad man, and certainly didn't deserve to be murdered. I want to help in any way I can to catch whoever did this."

"I understand." Faye nodded. "You mentioned earlier that he wasn't faithful. What did you mean?"

George pursed his lips, frowning. "He couldn't practice what he preached." His voice took on a sterner tone as he spoke. "A few months ago, I came here to put flowers on our mother's grave, and I popped in to see him. As I opened the door to his study, I found him in"—he paused—"in an awkward situation with a woman."

"Oh. I see," Faye said, her cheeks flushing slightly. "Do you know who the woman was?"

"I'm not sure. I didn't hang around to find out. Roger caught up with me a few moments later and asked me not to say anything, as she was married. He must have thought I recognized her."

There was a loud crash in the church hall, along with raised voices, and George sighed. "I better go and sort that out. Can you find your own way out?"

"Of course," Faye replied and left, clutching the hymn book with the note tucked carefully inside.

As soon as she was back home, she laid the hymn book on the kitchen table. Fanning the pages slowly, she started looking for anything else that might be a clue.

She gasped as she discovered there were two more notes hidden inside the hymn book on different pages.

The first said, "Meet me after hymn practice. Four o'clock."

"What have you got there?" Daniel interrupted while she was deep in thought. He picked up the second note. "'Tomorrow morning, eight thirty. Can't wait to see you, my love. M.'"

Daniel turned to Faye with a surprised look on his face.

"Well, you're a dark horse, Auntie Faye! You have a secret lover?" His face now broke into a wide smile.

"No, not me, Daniel," she corrected hastily. "The vicar."

"The vicar!" he exclaimed, rather too loudly, in Faye's opinion.

She quickly took the note back from Daniel and placed it back on the page of the hymn she'd found it on. "I need to get this to Inspector Rawlings."

"Who is 'M.'?" he asked.

"I don't know, but I mean to find out," she said, putting the hymn book back in her handbag. "Would you mind starting tea? I'm just going to pop down to the station to see if the inspector is there."

"No problem. Buster and I have it under control," he said and went to get the sausages from the refrigerator. Buster got up and stretched. Walking over to Daniel, he sat down, wagging his tail, and looked up expectantly, watching the string of sausages and Daniel's every move.

CHAPTER FOURTEEN

The Notes

Inspector Rawlings was surprised to see Faye at the police station.

"Hello, Miss Lantern, what can I do for you today?"

Seeing him in a plain white shirt with his sleeves rolled up, Faye was thrown for a minute. She was used to seeing him dressed in his dark jacket and overcoat, and it was a pleasant surprise to see him so relaxed and informal. For the first time, she noticed his bright blue eyes and felt herself having to look away, hoping he didn't notice her staring at him for a little longer than was necessary.

She carefully pulled the hymn book out of her handbag and handed it to him as she sat down.

"I was retrieving my scarf that I left at the vicarage, when I bumped into the vicar's brother, George."

Inspector Rawlings nodded, showing he was still listening as he looked at the hymn book, turning it over in his hand.

"I had a rather interesting conversation with him. He said that the vicar was having an affair with a married woman and had asked George not to say anything."

He looked up suddenly, focusing on Faye with interest. "Was he, indeed! And did he say who this married woman was, that the vicar was having the affair with?"

"Sadly, no," Faye said, leaning back disappointedly. "George didn't see who she was, but," she added, leaning forward again more excitedly and pointing to the hymn book, "there is a note . . . three, actually, written by an 'M.'"

He fanned through the book until he found the notes, careful not to lose the pages they were in as he read the words.

"'Tomorrow morning, eight thirty. M.'" He looked up at Faye. "So, this mysterious 'M.' could have been meeting the vicar at the time of his murder, putting them squarely in the frame."

Faye nodded silently.

"There's no date on it," he said, turning the note over to check the other side. And no one with the name 'M' springs to mind."

She could see the frustration in his face as he placed the note back in the book.

"I'll look into it. Thank you, Miss Lantern. As always, you have been most helpful and very timely, indeed. This will aid the investigation." He stopped abruptly, checking his watch before adding, "And help with the interview, which I need to attend now, as a matter of fact." He jumped up, grabbing his jacket off the back of his chair.

He stopped momentarily. "I'll pop by tomorrow, then."

Caught off guard, she stared at him vaguely.

With a twinkle in his eye, he smiled. "To finish our game of chess."

"Oh. Yes. Of course."

"I'll say good day to you, then."

"Yes. Good day, Inspector," she said, as she stood up and watched him stride out of the room, on his way to interview Rosemary, who was now in custody.

CHAPTER FIFTEEN

The Interview

Rosemary shifted nervously in her chair. Sitting alone, her eyes trailed around the shabby, square walls of the interview room. Four chairs sat wearily in faded blue material around the table in the middle where she now sat. Shivering from the cold and trembling, she lifted the glass of water that had been placed in front of her with both hands to steady it, as a tall, well-dressed man in a dark gray suit came marching in. He had wavy, slightly scruffy blond hair that framed his boyish-looking face. He sat down opposite her, dropping a file, which landed with a thud on the table in front of her. She noticed his youthful appearance didn't seem to match his serious demeanor as he started to talk.

"I'm Detective Inspector Rawlings. Do you know why you are here, Mrs. Bulmer?"

Rosemary sat silently; her head lowered. She looked up and met the cold stare of his steely blue eyes focused upon her, making her stomach lurch in fear. His face stern and unyielding, she felt trapped, like an animal without escape, as her eyes flicked over to the burly officer by the door barring the way and back to the inspector. Tears started to flood down her cheeks.

"I want to call my mother. I want her to be here with me," she said, half-shouting as she became more distressed.

"All in good time, Mrs. Bulmer. But first, I need you to tell me where you were on the morning of the seventeenth of September, between the hours of eight and ten o'clock?"

Rosemary's eyes glazed over with tears again, remembering that fateful morning.

"I . . . I was cleaning, at the vicarage," she stammered.

"So, you admit you were at the vicarage when the murder of Roger Pennell took place." His voice became more confrontational as he spoke.

She could feel the palms of her hands sweating as she replied nervously, "I was cleaning out the store cupboard at the far end of the church."

"Do you have any witnesses to corroborate that?"

She could feel her heart pounding in her chest, and she struggled to breathe as she replied, "No . . . I was on my own. I didn't hear anything."

"Nothing at all?" he quizzed, a slight mocking tone in his voice.

Before he could ask another question, the interview room door opened and a police officer walked in, holding a box containing a pair of black stiletto shoes. Rosemary gripped her hands together so tightly she could feel the pain of her nails digging into her skin as the officer closed the interview room door behind himself.

"Are these your shoes, Mrs. Bulmer?" the inspector asked, taking them out of the box and holding them up for her to see.

She glanced briefly at the shoes and felt a sudden jolt of sickness in her stomach. Memories of the day of the murder came flooding back, etched in the line of gray mud that clung to the sides of the black patent-leather shoes. She nodded slowly, her head now bowed again as he placed them back in the box.

"Do you wear them to work, Mrs. Bulman?"

She nodded again, in silence.

His voice rose to a surprised tone as he tried to provoke a reaction from her. "Do you always do the cleaning in your high heels?"

Even through his mocking tone, he had an authority and knowing about him that seemed to precede his years, and an uneasiness crept over her as she tried to choose the right words, that wouldn't open up another line of questioning from him, but she stumbled over her words instead, replying, "I change . . . I walk . . . I wear them to work, and then I change into my cleaning shoes."

Silently, he pulled a tattered hymn book out of his pocket and placed it on the table. Stifling a gasp, she masked a sharp intake of breath as he pulled out a note from inside the book and held it up.

"Did you write this note?"

Regaining her composure, she looked nonchalantly at the note as he placed it down on the table, sliding it toward her.

"That's not my initial. My initial is 'R.,'" she replied, still feigning disinterest, and looking away, she folded her arms.

A knock at the door interrupted them as another police officer walked in and whispered into Inspector Rawlings's ear, before standing back.

He nodded, thanking the officer, and turned back to look at her again. "Mrs. Bulman. We have just had confirmation that the fingerprints we found on the gravestone outside the vicarage are yours. Not only that, but your fingerprints were made up of Roger Pennell's blood!" He stopped deliberately, looking directly at her, and said in a grave tone, "Mrs. Bulman, can you explain how you came to have Roger Pennell's blood on your hands?"

His words echoed in her head, and she could feel her whole body start to tremble as he paused, staring at her, waiting for a reply. For a moment, she sensed in him a genuine feeling of sadness for her, his face softening as he said gently, "This is your last chance to cooperate and tell us the truth, Rosemary. Did you kill Roger Pennell?"

Terrified, confused, and unable to speak, she watched as he picked up the pair of shoes in the box again, and holding them up, his voice grew stern once more.

"These shoes, which you have confirmed belong to you, have traces of blood on them, Roger Pennell's blood."

Rosemary let out a desperate scream. "No! It wasn't me!"

The two police officers in the room rushed forward on each side of Rosemary, holding her arms to restrain her as she tried to stand up. She froze, as Inspector Rawlings paused and drew in a deep breath before speaking again in a slow, deliberate tone.

"We also have confirmation that the fingerprints found on the flowerpot that was used to kill Dorothy Mahoney were also yours."

"No. I didn't kill her!" she screamed, sick to her stomach as he continued.

"Mrs. Bulmer, I am arresting you for the murders of Dorothy Mahoney and Roger Pennell. You do not have to say anything, but if you do say anything, it can be used as evidence against you in a court of law. Do you understand?"

She started screaming uncontrollably, and the two offices struggled to hold her in the chair before finally handcuffing her hands behind her back.

"Take her away!" the inspector said, standing up. "This interview is over."

"It wasn't me. I didn't kill anyone. I loved Roger!" she cried, and the noise of her chair crashing to the floor was masked only by her screams as she was dragged away.

CHAPTER SIXTEEN

A Hunch

"It's a textbook case."

Inspector Rawlings was sipping tea and put his cup down on the saucer as Faye replied, "Maybe?"

"You surely don't think she's innocent?" he said, staring back at her.

Faye grimaced at his words, absentmindedly twirling her hair at the back of her head into a coil with her finger as she was thinking. "What I don't understand," she said, "is why Rosemary would kill the vicar and then hold him in an embrace, if your theory is correct, when he was dying or even dead?"

He shrugged. "Who knows? Maybe she regretted murdering him after she had done the deed."

"But what was the motive, Inspector?"

He thought for a moment. "If, as I suspect, she was having an affair with Roger Pennell, and she tried to end the affair, he could have threatened to tell Greg?"

Faye shook her head. She wasn't convinced. "Did she admit to killing him?"

"No. She denied it," he replied, placing his saucer on the floor with a tea-soaked biscuit on it for Buster.

She gasped. "You'll get us both in trouble," she said as she looked around for the inevitable dressing down from the owner of the tea shop. It was a fancy tea shop a few villages down, and the owner, an elegant woman in her fifties with her dark hair tied neatly in a bun, seemed to watch their every move. Faye had accepted a lift from the inspector, who was driving out that way. She was on an errand to pick up a book for Daniel, who was working, and she had agreed to have a brief tea break with the inspector before their drive back. She was now wondering whether it was such a good idea.

The inspector, sensing her distress, said, "I'll take the blame, if anything's said." He knew keeping on Buster's good side was the better of the two options.

"The thing is, Miss Lantern," he continued, "as I said before, the facts don't lie. Rosemary was at the scene of the crime. Her fingerprints were on the gravestone and the vicar's blood was on her shoes. It's undeniable evidence."

"What about Dollie Mahoney's murder?" she asked, watching him take a bite of his third tea cake.

"Rosemary's fingerprints were on the flowerpot that was used to hit Dollie over the head and kill her. It puts her at the scene with the murder weapon in her hand. It's irrefutable evidence," he added.

Faye picked up the small pot of cream on the table and started spreading it on her scone.

"Did you find out who the footprint at Mrs. Mahoney's cottage belonged to?"

"We found a match," he replied, taking another sip of tea. "When we took Rosemary's shoes from the house for testing, they were in the hallway next to Greg's. We took his boot for testing, and they were a match for the print at Dollie's cottage. A size nine with the same pattern of wear in their markings."

"Well, surely, that puts him at the murder scene with Dollie?" she exclaimed.

"In our investigation, it appears he was a regular visitor at Mrs. Mahoney's cottage, so it's no surprise that the footprints match."

She shook her head. She knew that something wasn't adding up, she just couldn't put her finger on it.

"Have you interviewed Greg . . . Mr. Bulmer?"

"We've not managed to catch up with him yet."

Faye's suspicion was growing. "I think he is a part of this."

"But where is the evidence?" he asked her.

She slumped back in her chair. Of course, Inspector Rawlings was right, but she wasn't about to give up that easily.

"Inspector, would you mind if I visited Mrs. Bulmer?"

He went to object, but Faye jumped in ahead of him.

"It would put my mind at rest," she added.

He thought for a moment, folding his napkin and placing it on his plate. "If it really helps you to have peace of mind, Miss Lantern, to put this whole business behind you."

"Thank you, Inspector. That's very kind of you." She stood up. "I would like to see her now, if you don't mind."

"Now! You want to go now?" he said with surprise.

"Yes, please."

The inspector stood up from the table. "What about Buster?" he asked, trying to catch up with Faye, who was already walking toward the door.

"I'll drop him home on the way. Come on," she called, and Inspector Rawlings wasn't sure if she was talking to Buster or him as he followed her out the door.

CHAPTER SEVENTEEN

The Missing Pieces

The police station was particularly busy as Faye arrived with Inspector Rawlings. She sat down on the only chair and moved into the corner, away from the two men arguing with a constable at the front desk, as she awaited the return of the inspector, who reappeared a few minutes later, waving for Faye to come over.

The desk sergeant, who had just finished a telephone conversation, was writing some notes down and stopped the inspector as they were about to go through to the interview room.

"That was Mrs. Malvern, Rosemary Bulmer's mother. She said she wanted to come in to see her daughter and is on her way."

Inspector Rawlings nodded and took the note from him.

"I'll be right outside, Miss Lantern. You have five minutes to put your mind at rest."

Faye nodded, her stomach turning in knots as she started to second-guess herself and wondered whether she was doing the right thing or not.

Rosemary looked at Faye, studying her face as she walked in. Faye pulled the chair out from under the table. The noise of the feet dragging along the floor cut through the silence.

She noticed how drawn and tired Rosemary looked. Her skin was sallow, her eyes puffy from crying. She sat with her shoulders slumped, her small, thin frame hunched over the table.

“Hello, Rosemary, I’m Faye Lantern,” she said, looking directly at Rosemary. “I’ve just moved into the Old Station House and unfortunately, I was the one who discovered the vicar’s body.”

Rosemary looked up. She was visibly shaken, as though reliving a memory as Faye spoke.

“I believe you are innocent and want to help you. Are you able to answer a few questions?”

“What kind of questions?” she asked, with an air of caution in her voice.

“I wanted to ask you how you felt about Roger . . . the vicar?”

Rosemary looked surprised, Faye’s question catching her off guard. “I loved him!” she said, her hands now covering her face as she began sobbing again.

Faye waited quietly for her to compose herself and bring her hands down from her face before asking her, "Can you tell me what happened?"

Rosemary hung her head down again for a few seconds, before eventually looking back at Faye. "I didn't kill him. I found him," she stammered. "He was on the floor, there was blood everywhere . . . He was already dead," she sobbed.

"Did you see anyone there?"

Faye noticed Rosemary paused for a moment, a flash of despair in her eyes before answering, "No. No, I didn't see anyone else there."

At that moment, Inspector Rawlings opened the door and strode over to address Rosemary. "Your mother is here."

Faye noticed a look of hope in Rosemary's eyes as her mother walked in.

"Mother!" Rosemary exclaimed and burst into tears again as her mother rushed over, throwing her arms around Rosemary to comfort her.

"This has all been a terrible mistake," she said, turning to Inspector Rawlings. "My Mary wouldn't hurt a fly!"

"Please take a seat, Mrs. Malvern," he said, ignoring her pleas, "I'm afraid the evidence tells another story." And with that, he ushered Faye out of the room.

Faye stopped suddenly.

"Are you alright, Miss Lantern?"

"Mary!" she said aloud. "She called her Mary!"

"Yes. It's quite common for someone to be called by an abbreviation of their name," the inspector said matter-of-factly.

Faye turned to Inspector Rawlings. "But don't you see? 'M.' She was using her shortened name on the note. No one knew her as Mary."

"I can't see what you are getting at, Miss Lantern. Even if that was her signing as 'M.'"

"Well, Inspector, if Rosemary is 'M.,' she professes her love for the vicar in the note and asks to meet him at nine o'clock in the morning."

The inspector nodded. "Yes, that was on the note in the hymn book."

Faye continued, "Rosemary has already said she left for work at eight o'clock. The vicar was murdered between eight and ten o'clock, and Rosemary was meeting him at nine o'clock. Which means the vicar could have already been murdered before Rosemary arrived at eight thirty."

The inspector nodded silently in thought for a moment before replying, "It's a long shot, but there's still no evidence to substantiate your theory, Miss Lantern."

"Not yet, Inspector," she replied. "But it is possible."

Which she knew Inspector Rawlings couldn't discount.

Faye went home and all that afternoon, her mind was churning, looking for answers, until she could take it no more.

"Buster!" she called. "Let's go and feed the ducks!" And with that, Faye set off with Buster springing along beside her until she reached the ducks by the canal. The fresh air cleared her head, and as she arrived back home, she was met with the smell of bacon being cooked as she walked in.

"I hope you don't mind, Auntie Faye. I missed lunch and I'm starving!" Daniel was taking a bite of his bacon sandwich, accompanied by Buster, who was already by his side, with long dribbles of drool hanging from each side of his mouth.

"Oh. I forgot to say. A man dropped off this letter," Daniel said, handing Faye a small brown envelope. Faye opened the envelope to see a handwritten note from George, letting her know the time of the vicar's funeral and inviting her to attend. She put it to the side, as the image of the vicar's dead body flashed up in her mind.

"Are you alright? You look a little pale," Daniel called out from the kitchen.

"I'm fine. It's just the thought of attending the funeral," she replied.

"Do you have to go? I'm sure no one will mind—they'll understand it might be traumatic for you, bringing it all back up," he added, scraping the leftover scraps of bacon into Buster's bowl.

Faye straightened up. "No. I'll be there tomorrow, to pay my respects. I will feel better knowing I have done that."

She slumped down in the armchair by the fire and closed her eyes, part of her wondering if Petworth was all she had hoped for, as its charm had started to wear off a little.

CHAPTER EIGHTEEN

The Wake

The rain came down hard, pummeling the row of black umbrellas lined around the graveside, until the noise reached a deafening crescendo, enough to drown out Reverend Fallow's last words as the vicar's coffin was being lowered into the grave.

Faye was relieved as the group started to disperse, quickly making their way to the village hall, bracing against the rain with their heads down and struggling to hold their umbrellas against the relentless wind.

Inside the hall, Faye looked around to see Gwen standing at a table that stretched across the back of the hall. It was covered in a pristine white tablecloth that draped down, just covering the top of the table legs. There were pots of tea and plates loaded with cakes and biscuits dotted around next to platters of sandwiches and small pastries. Gwen was moving trays about to make room for the plate she had just brought over when she spotted Faye. Waving, she rushed over.

"Margie's here!" were the first words out of her mouth. "Can you believe it? After all that business of being arrested!"

Faye started to realize Gwen was a good source of local knowledge, but also the local gossip, and made a mental note not to share too much with her about her personal life.

"Faye. I'm so glad you could make it." George seemed a welcome relief and Faye smiled, acknowledging him.

"I'm off to finish putting out the sausage rolls," Gwen announced and disappeared into the gathering crowd.

George turned to Faye. "How are you?"

"Well. Thank you, George. I can't imagine this has been an easy day for you."

"I'm glad to have the opportunity to say my goodbyes," he said, and lifted his hand to his eyes, brushing away a tear as he spoke. He shuffled about from one foot to another for a moment, clearing his throat and collecting himself again, just in time as a very well-dressed couple joined them.

"Hello, George, darling," came the smooth, sultry voice. Her blue eyes and dark red lipstick were striking under a wide-brimmed black hat and long, dark brown fur coat. An equally smart silver-haired man, with a slightly care worn but tanned face, was standing next to her in a sharply cut black suit and tie.

"Elizabeth," George replied, kissing her on both cheeks before turning to the man and shaking his hand. "Edmund. I wasn't sure you would be back in time."

"We changed our flight to come back a day early."

George nodded. "I appreciate your presence here today. It means a lot."

"We're glad we can be here to support a dear friend."

George smiled. "Have you met Faye? She has just moved into the Old Station House."

"Darling!" Elizabeth moved in to kiss Faye on the cheek. Body tense, Faye awkwardly acknowledged her and stepped back.

"How are you finding our neck of the woods, Faye?" Edmund interrupted, with a friendly but upper-class tone to his voice as he spoke.

Elizabeth jumped in before Faye could answer.

"Edmund. There have been two murders here in the last week! The poor darling hasn't had a chance to see the best of us yet!"

Faye was silent for a moment before replying, "Well, I have met some wonderful people." She turned to George, smiling. "So, it's not all bad!"

"Oh, thank goodness we haven't put you off staying just yet." Elizabeth laughed and turned to George. "Would you be a dear and fetch me a glass of sherry?"

She handed George her empty glass, and he headed off toward the buffet table as she turned to face Faye.

"I wanted to speak with you, without George here," she continued. "I didn't feel it was the right thing to do, to mention the vicar's—Roger's murder in front of him. Especially today," she added, half-looking around the room and then back at Faye. Lowering her voice, she said, "I heard you discovered Roger's body. I can't imagine how awful that must have been for you, darling."

Faye nodded, her stomach turning again as the image of the vicar lying in a pool of blood came back. "Yes. It was quite a shock," she replied, noticing Elizabeth for the first time looked a little more serious.

"And of all the people, the inspector has arrested Rosemary Bulmer! I just can't believe Rosemary murdered poor Roger. She always seemed such a sweet little thing."

"I would have put my money on it being her husband Greg, if it was anyone," Edmund added.

"You think it was Greg?" Faye said with interest, looking at Edmund.

"Well," he said, "we were on our way to the train station to pick up some friends, before going to the airport for our holiday, and we saw Greg going into the church."

Faye's eyes lit up. "On the day of the murder?" she asked eagerly.

"Yes. It was," he replied.

"Can you remember what time you saw him going into the church?"

"Oh. I think it was about eight fifteen in the morning." He looked over at Elizabeth for confirmation.

"Yes," Elizabeth agreed. "Definitely no later, as we had to be at the train station for eight forty-five, to pick up our friends, and we always like to be early."

Faye could not contain her surprise at hearing this news and asked, "Have you spoken with Inspector Rawlings yet?"

Edmund jumped in again. "Golly! We haven't had much time. Only arrived back today, you see, just in time for the funeral. We were planning on speaking with the inspector after we made sure George was okay and we had paid our respects."

"Of course," Faye said. "But I think you have vital information that the inspector needs to hear."

“My goodness! Do you really think it’s that important?” Elizabeth asked.

“Most definitely.”

“Well, there’s no time like the present,” Edmund added.

“But what about George?” she asked, turning back to Edmund.

“I can stay with George,” Faye offered. “I’ll let him know you had urgent business to attend to.”

“Right! Jolly good!” Edmund said, jumping into action. “We’ll say our goodbyes and pop up to the station to see Inspector Rawlings.”

“Darling, it was lovely to meet you,” Elizabeth said. “You must pop in for lunch sometime.”

“I would love to.” Faye smiled and watched them leave. It wasn’t long before more people followed behind them, and the hall started to empty, until there was only Faye and George left behind.

“It was good of you to stay,” George said, turning to Faye.

“Not at all,” Faye replied. “As funerals go, I think it was a great success. If you don’t mind me saying,” she added quickly.

George laughed. "Yes, it was a good day. I think we did Roger proud."

"Do you need a hand with the clearing up?" she asked him.

"Thank you, Faye, but I think Gwen has it covered; she's nearly done." Looking back at Faye, he added, "I believe I need to go home and rest awhile. It's been a long day." He smiled. "Thank you again for coming. I hope I can help or offer you the same support you have shown me if you ever need it."

Faye nodded. "Thank you. That's kind of you to say." Then she left George behind as she walked out of the hall, deep in thought about how the conversation between Edmund, Elizabeth, and Inspector Rawlings was unfolding.

CHAPTER NINETEEN

Betrayal

Faye was enjoying the early morning sun as she attempted to clip the pink roses that framed the arbor archway at the side of the Station House.

"Good morning, Miss Lantern." Inspector Rawlings came into view, hat in hand as he arrived at the front gate of the Station House.

Buster leapt up from the hole he had been digging under the tree to greet the inspector, who had hastily lowered his hat out of sight.

"Hello, Buster. How are you today?" he asked, retrieving a biscuit from his pocket and handing it to Buster, who was standing on two legs, tail wagging, at the gate.

Faye laughed quietly to herself as she watched the scene unfold. Buster seemed to get the best out of people, usually resulting in a treat coming his way, in one way or another.

"Good morning, Inspector. I was just about to put the kettle on. Would you care for a cup of tea?"

"Thank you, Miss Lantern," he replied, walking briskly down the path, then following Faye inside with Buster close behind. Buster seemed to know that there would be more biscuits on the horizon.

The inspector sat down and studied the chessboard. "Umm," he muttered, and then a few minutes later, another, "Umm," before finally spotting his move. Feeling rather pleased with the outcome after moving his rook, he sat back.

"Are you here on official business, Inspector?" Faye asked, placing the tea tray on the table. The inspector was glad for the opportunity to call in on Faye, who always seemed to have a steady flow of tea and biscuits on hand.

"Well, Miss Lantern," he said, leaning forward again, choosing his favorite custard creams from the plate of biscuits. "I've had a very interesting conversation with the Percys, Edmund and Elizabeth, from the Manor House."

"Yes. I met them yesterday at the funeral," she replied.

The inspector nodded. "You'll be pleased to know they have brought some new evidence to light. I have a sworn statement from them saying they saw Greg Bulmer going into the vicarage on the morning of the vicar's murder, which now makes Greg Bulmer a person of great interest to us."

"You haven't managed to find Greg yet?" Faye asked, pouring the tea.

"He has evaded us up to now. But, in light of this new evidence, we will be stepping up the search for him. I've put extra men on it."

Faye thought about Rosemary and what Elizabeth had said about her frailness.

"What I don't understand, Inspector," she said, stirring her tea, "is, if Greg murdered the vicar, Rosemary would know, I'm sure. But she hasn't said anything. Why would she protect him?"

"That's what I was wondering," he said, trying to keep Buster's drooling away from his trouser leg. "She is on a double murder charge. It doesn't add up."

Faye was still thinking about what the inspector had said, long after he had left. If there was a secret someone in the village was hiding, who might know about it? She grabbed her coat from the stand by the front door and with Buster at her side, walked down to the green. On the way back, she stopped at the bakery. Gwen smiled as she saw Faye and Buster walk in.

"The usual?" she said, holding up a loaf of sliced bread for Faye to see.

"Yes. Thank you," Faye called out as she took her purse out to pay.

Gwen placed the carefully wrapped loaf on the counter. “I thought the vicar’s funeral went well yesterday,” she said, dusting the flour off her apron.

Faye nodded. “I think it helped George to have so much support from everyone.”

“I like to think we all stick together in the village,” Gwen replied, before adding, “Even the Percys showed up, and”—she lowered her voice to a whisper, looking around—“dropped a bombshell!”

“A bombshell?” Faye repeated.

Gwen leaned in toward Faye as she spoke. “Yes. They saw Rosemary’s husband, Greg, going into the church at the time the vicar was murdered,” she said, wide-eyed.

“Oh!” said Faye. “How do you know that?”

“There’s not much that gets by me,” she replied, straightening up as she spoke, and Faye didn’t doubt it for a minute. “I always knew he was a baddun.”

“What do you mean?” Faye asked, placing the loaf in her bag and handing Gwen a sixpence.

Gwen leaned in toward Faye again and, half-whispering, said, “He wouldn’t let Rosemary see her baby boy. When they first met, he worked at the London Hostel.” She lowered her voice again. “Where girls that get pregnant are sent,” she mouthed, “if they are unmarried.”

A look of sadness fell across Gwen's face. "Rosemary was my best friend at school. I was the only one that she confided in. I remember how happy she was the day she told me Greg was going to marry her and say the baby was his." Gwen sighed. "But he went back on his word after they were married. He told her he didn't want anything to do with another man's child and wouldn't let Rosemary see her son."

A few customers came in for orders and left again before Gwen continued.

"Rosemary became ill and wouldn't eat. She became depressed and ended up in hospital. Her mother was so concerned for her that she agreed to take Archie, Rosemary's baby boy, and say he was adopted, so that he could live with her and Rosemary could see him now and again.

"Of course, it was a big secret," she said. "No one knows about it except for me."

After listening to Gwen's account of the story, Faye could feel the threads coming together.

She waited patiently for Gwen to serve a few more customers with bread and scones, before carrying on the conversation.

"So, Rosemary was protecting her son's identity and her mother's reputation as the grandmother," she said, as the noise of the till closing rang out. "Because she knew

Greg would tell everyone the truth and ruin her mother's life, along with her son's and her own." Now it made sense. "Thank you, Gwen, for sharing that. I think it may help Rosemary if the inspector knows about it. Would you mind me sharing what you have told me with the inspector, for Rosemary's sake?"

Gwen thought for a moment. "For Rosemary's sake. Then I suppose so. But please tell him to keep it quiet and not to let the press hear of it."

Faye nodded. "Most definitely." She looked at Gwen. "You are a good friend, Gwen, and Rosemary may well have you to thank for helping her right now." Which, Faye noticed, seemed to put Gwen's mind at ease. She had done the right thing to tell Faye, whom she seemed to have put her trust in.

CHAPTER TWENTY

Intuition

Inspector Rawlings sat at his desk, taking in all that Faye had recounted to him.

"So, you think she is scared Greg Bulmer will tell her secret and ruin her and her mother's good standing. That's why she's protecting him."

"Exactly," Faye replied.

"But that still doesn't explain Dollie's murder," he said, and Faye couldn't disagree.

"Inspector, maybe speaking to Rosemary on your own, to tell her you know about her son, Archie, may help her in telling you what really happened, as she won't have much to lose anymore."

"It's worth a try. But we would still need evidence."

Faye thought about the footprints from Greg's boots that were found at Dollie's cottage. "I believe, Inspector, you may find the evidence you need at Greg's own home."

"How so?" he asked.

"If Greg murdered the vicar, he would surely have some blood stains on his clothes. You took Rosemary into custody almost immediately, so she wouldn't have had a chance to wash them, and maybe Greg forgot about them, as you had already arrested Rosemary and he thought he was in the clear."

The inspector picked up the telephone on his desk before Faye had finished speaking.

"This is Inspector Rawlings—I want a team ready to search Greg Bulmer's house in thirty minutes."

Faye stood up and left the inspector's office, feeling more at ease. Her intuition had led her one step closer to finding out the truth about what had happened. She only hoped that the inspector would find his evidence.

CHAPTER TWENTYONE

Devil's Fire

Inspector Rawlings had put posters up at the police station and around the village asking anyone to report a sighting of Greg Bulmer. He was hopeful that if Greg was in the village, someone would spot him and report it to the police. After two weeks, no one came forward with any information and Faye was losing hope that Greg would be found. The inspector assumed he had "skipped town," but Faye was still desperate to help Rosemary, as she was certain she hadn't committed either of the murders, and prayed that something would turn up.

It was two o'clock in the afternoon when the telephone rang, and Daniel called out to Faye, who had started tackling the Roses again, that Mrs. Field was on the telephone.

"Mrs. Field? Whatever can she want?" Faye asked out loud, to which Daniel shrugged his shoulders as he left to meet a new client at work.

"Hello, Mrs. Field. How can I help you?"

"There are some funny goings on next door," she replied abruptly. "Strange bumps and bangs in the night—at Dollie's cottage next door."

"Oh," Faye replied.

"I saw a candle for a few seconds," she added. "It just lit the window and disappeared—I think there are squatters in there!"

"What makes you say that?" Faye asked.

"There were some hippie-type travelers camping in the fields down the lane a few days ago," she explained. "They probably saw the cottage was empty and decided to move in." She sounded quite satisfied with her deduction of the situation.

"I see," Faye replied. "Do you mind me asking why you are telling me and not Inspector Rawlings?"

"I wouldn't speak to the inspector if he was the last man on earth!" came the answer, Margie's voice now shaking in anger as she spoke. "He is a complete imbecile! He arrested me and humiliated me, and I will get my revenge."

The line went quiet for a moment before she continued. "I know you speak with him, and I don't want squatters living next door to me. You don't know what diseases they are spreading!"

Faye could sense the fear in her and spoke calmly, trying to reassure her. "I understand, Mrs. Field. Would you like me to pass the message on for you?"

"If you think it's worthwhile," she said defensively. "Though I'm sure he won't bother investigating."

"Okay, Mrs. Field. Leave it with me," Faye added and hung up.

Living on her own, Faye realized Mrs. Field might be feeling vulnerable, not knowing who was in Dollie's home, especially after the recent events, and decided to call the inspector. She left a message.

Faye was heading past Dollie's cottage later that afternoon to post a letter to her sister.

While she waited for the inspector to call her back, and to see if she could put Mrs. Field's mind at rest, she decided to just take a quick look herself.

She left the post office and headed down the lane toward Dollie's cottage. She could see the "hippies," as Mrs. Field had called them, camped in the paddock behind Dollie's cottage, and she understood her reasoning. It was daylight still, and Faye thought it could do no harm to have a look from the outside of Dollie's cottage. She walked along the front path and peered in through the window. She couldn't see anything out of the ordinary. There was an armchair and sofa to either side of the fireplace and a small table to the side with a vase standing in the middle of it. She followed the path to the back gate, and unlatching the gate handle, walked around the side of the cottage to the back door, which Faye noticed wasn't locked as she tried the handle. Before she realized it, she had stepped one foot inside the kitchen. She couldn't hear anything and stepped further in. Looking around the kitchen, she noticed a few plates and cutlery piled up in the sink. She made her way silently down the hallway, and stopped, peering around the door and into the front room she had seen from the outside. It looked neat and tidy, except for a few books and a newspaper that were lying on the floor. As Faye moved closer in, she could see a map under a pile of books. She bent down and pulled the map out, opening it up as she stood, balancing it across the top of the chair. Looking closely, she could see a route marked out in red pen, running along the old bridle path leading on to the next village.

A creaking noise startled her, making her turn and look around—to see Greg Bulmer standing there. His sunken eyes peered eerily out at her from under a mop of greasy dark hair that clung limply to one side of his face. His shirt marked with stains, his disheveled appearance betraying the squalid existence he had been living for the past few weeks. Her eyes darted to the door behind him, which was now closed. She could feel her heart pounding but tried not letting fear show in her voice as she spoke.

"Greg! There you are," she said in a light-hearted tone. "We have all been so worried about you."

She saw his jaw tense as he gritted his teeth, his stubbled face dark and his demeanor menacing as he spoke.

"You've been poking your nose in things that you have no business in."

He took a step nearer to Faye.

"You should have left things alone."

Faye knew she needed to escape, and her mind raced for any idea to help her out of the situation.

"I wanted to help Rosemary," she blurted out, thinking he cared about Rosemary and hearing her name would help to soften him, but it had the opposite effect. He flew into a rage at the sound of her name, smashing the vase on the table across the floor as he grabbed Faye by the throat with one hand, pinning her to the dining room wall.

"She made a fool of me. That Jezebel was sleeping with Roger Pennell," he snarled, now so close to Faye she could feel his breath on her face. With both hands trying to pull his arm away, she struggled, starting to lose consciousness. Greg loosened his grip, and she gasped for air; her hands dropping down, she placed them flat on the back of the wall to steady herself. She stood motionless, still gasping to breathe as he stepped away from her and walked over to the chair, gathering up the opened map.

"I gave her everything," he said, turning back to Faye with a sudden look of sadness in his eyes. "All that any woman could want. Even letting her see that brat of a child, but oh, no, that wasn't enough for her."

He stuffed the folded map angrily into his pocket. "She had to humiliate me, too. Well, I wasn't going to let them get away with it, not her or the vicar or Dollie."

"Dollie?" she replied fearfully, feeling panic start to rise in her again as Greg's eyes narrowed, focusing on her as he spoke.

"She was going to let everyone know about Rosemary's affair with the vicar if he didn't make sure she won the Best in Bloom cup." He paused. "So, I stopped her little game." He smiled, a sickly smile, darkness creeping into his eyes.

Faye pressed back harder on the wall in fear as he glared at her.

"I had it all planned, and it was going well, until you started interfering."

She looked around the room, searching for a way out, but Greg followed her gaze, his eyes staring intently at her, his voice now eerily calm as he spoke.

"I watched Rosemary cry over his dead body when she found him. Now, she can pay for what she did to me. She can rot in a jail somewhere, that's her penance."

Faye knew time was running out as she said, "You don't have to do this. Just let me go. I won't say anything."

Greg's face had glazed over, his vacant expression unnerving as his mind seemed to have drifted to another place.

She realized if she didn't act now, it would be her demise. Grabbing the poker stick from the fireplace next to her left leg, she held it up with both hands to defend herself.

A cruel smile spread across Greg's face as he pulled a lighter from his pocket, and bending down, lit the cotton tassels of the round floral-patterned cushion that lay between them on the floor.

Faye gasped in horror. "What are you doing?"

"Getting rid of loose ends." He smirked.

She went to run, but Greg moved forward blocking her way. She watched, terrified, as Greg picked up a newspaper from the floor and scattered its pages on to the burning cushion. The fire took off, flames leaping up and onto the small wooden table Greg had kicked over. He pulled at the armchair, dragging it onto the fire, and Faye started to cough, dropping to her knees as plumes of black smoke started to billow out into the room. Greg backed away to the door, waiting until the smoke was too thick to see through. Faye heard the opening and closing of the dining room door as it slammed shut behind him. Gasping for air, she started crawling along the floor. She knew the window was near, but she was unable to see where she was going. The noise of smashing glass filled the room then, and Faye heard Inspector Rawlings's frantic voice calling out.

"Miss Lantern, Miss Lantern, are you in there?"

"Inspector," she called back, coughing again. She could see a flashlight shine down on her outstretched hand and felt herself being pulled up to the window before passing out.

Faye woke up to see Inspector Rawlings sitting in the chair opposite her hospital bed, half asleep. Noticing Faye was awake, he jumped up.

"Miss Lantern. You gave us quite a scare."

Faye could see the concern etched on his face.

"I'm so sorry, Inspector. I didn't know Greg was in the cottage. Have you arrested him?" she asked, suddenly feeling fearful.

Faye noticed the inspector's brow crease into lines as he frowned. "We gave chase, but he evaded my men as he ran into the woods. But rest assured, we will get him."

Faye nodded. "He admitted to murdering the vicar and Dollie."

Inspector Rawlings studied Faye's face as he asked, "He told you that?"

She nodded. "He said that he watched Rosemary cry when she found the vicar's dead body and that he had put a stop to Dollie's little game. She had threatened to expose Rosemary's affair with the vicar. I don't think he was expecting me to get out alive to tell anyone that," she added, feeling a little shaky as she remembered the fire. "Thank you, Inspector. For saving me. I . . . I . . ." Her words faltered.

The inspector, seeing her distress, said, "You have Mrs. Field to thank for your rescue. She notified us that she heard a smash and came over to investigate. That's when she saw Greg in the room with you through the window, with his hand at your throat." The inspector paused before adding quietly, "That must have been quite an ordeal for you."

Faye recoiled as she remembered Greg's breath on her face and how afraid she had been.

Sensing her uneasiness, the inspector interrupted her thoughts. "We'll catch him. You can rest assured of that."

His face softened, and he paused, as if going to say something to Faye, then straightening up, said instead, "I'll leave you in peace now, Miss Lantern. I'm going to speak with Rosemary again and see what she has to say, now I have all this new information."

Faye smiled, pleased that Rosemary now had a chance of being set free. "Thank you, Inspector," she called out as he was leaving.

He lifted his hat. "Just doing my job." Then he strode out the room as he so often did, with his coattails flying out behind him. Faye now understood what Daniel had meant, when he said Inspector Rawlings's nickname in the village was Batman.

CHAPTER TWENTYTWO

Rosemary's Testimony

Faye sat in her armchair and took a deep breath and relaxed. It had been a few weeks since her incident with Greg, and she was still troubled by nightmares that frequently woke her in the early hours of the morning. Sitting in the chair, she heard Daniel's footsteps coming down the stairs and into the hallway, also noticed by Buster, who got up and stretched before jumping off his chair and trotting over to greet Daniel.

"How are you feeling today, Auntie Faye?" he asked, walking back with a bottle of milk from the doorstep.

"Much better, thank you."

"Good. Don't forget the inspector is coming round at eleven o'clock today."

"Is it today?" she said, alarmed at having forgotten something so simple that she would never normally forget.

"He's coming to finish the chess game," he added, nodding toward the half-played game still sitting on the table.

By the time breakfast was over, Faye just had time to tidy up. She couldn't abide mess and couldn't think straight if something was out of place.

Inspector Rawlings wiped his feet on the mat, hat already in hand as he stepped into the Old Station House.

"It looks very homely and welcoming in here," he said, gazing around the room.

Soft green curtains adorned the windows and thick, large gold, red, and green Persian rugs sprawled over wooden floors, creating a feeling of warmth. There were two large chairs sitting on either side of the fireplace, and nearby, a dining room table stood with a vase of brightly colored flowers, on a round crocheted doily in the center. A gleaming, highly polished piano and stool were nestled into the alcove at the far end of the room. Paintings dotted around hugged the walls, and one of a boat in the harbor, hanging above the fireplace, caught Inspector Rawlings's eye.

"That's a fine-looking painting," he remarked as he walked over to take a better look.

"Thank you," Faye said. "I painted that a few years ago."

"Oh," the inspector said, surprised. "A woman of many talents, then?" He smiled.

Faye laughed.

Turning to her, Rawlings said, “It’s good to see you looking so well. After all that business . . .” He didn’t finish his sentence.

“Thank you. Do you mind me asking what happened with Rosemary, Inspector?”

“Well,” he began, taking off his overcoat and hanging it over the back of the chair.

Faye resisted the urge to gather it up and hang it in its correct place on the coat stand by the front door.

“You were right,” he announced as they sat down. “Once I told Rosemary I knew about the baby, she broke down and testified that Greg had, in fact, murdered Dollie. He was still at Dollie’s house when Rosemary went to tackle her about blackmailing the vicar, as you had told me.”

Faye nodded, listening intently as the inspector continued.

“Greg heard Dollie and Rosemary’s conversation from outside and flew inside the shed in a rage.”

Faye felt herself recoil back in her chair as the inspector was talking, and she took a deep breath in to steady her nerves. She was uneasy that Greg was still on the loose. She heard the inspector’s voice again.

“Miss Lantern?”

"Sorry, I was just thinking about Dollie." She shook her head to clear it. "So, Rosemary and Greg's footprints were both at the scene of Dollie's murder, but only Rosemary's fingerprints were on the flowerpot that killed Dollie?" she said, puzzled.

The inspector nodded, leaning forward in his chair. "Rosemary said she had picked up the flowerpot in anger to smash it on the floor as she argued with Dollie, to show her that's what she thought of her precious flowers. But Greg took it from her and hit Dollie over the side of the head, smashing the flowerpot."

Faye shuddered, remembering the look of anger in Greg's eyes as he had flown toward *her* in a rage. She took a moment to recollect herself and push the image from her mind before asking, "But what about his fingerprints? Surely, they were on the flowerpot?"

"He was wearing gloves," the inspector explained. "Unbeknown to Rosemary, he had been cutting back some overgrown brambles around the back of the shed when she arrived. That's why she didn't see him."

Buster nudged Faye's leg gently, trying to get her attention as he jumped up and down, bouncing toward the kitchen and the tray of freshly made sandwiches that were sitting on the top, covered with a clean white teacloth.

"Just a minute, Buster," Faye called to him.

"The good news is, we found the evidence right where you suggested, at Greg and Rosemary's house. Greg had stuffed his gloves and trousers at the bottom of the laundry basket. Better still, we found traces of Dollie's blood on Greg's trousers and gloves."

Faye sighed with relief and added, "He probably thought as Rosemary had been arrested, he was in the clear, and didn't give it another thought. After all, you had all the evidence you needed with Rosemary's shoes and fingerprints. I think he got a bit cocky, thinking he was home free."

"And a stroke of luck for me!" Inspector Rawlings said. "That he got careless."

Faye nodded, glad that Rosemary had now been cleared and the charges dropped.

Inspector Rawlings's eyes widened as Faye fetched the sandwich tray and placed it down on the table. She had set aside a small bone in a bowl for Buster, who was sitting close to the inspector's leg, his eyes following the ham sandwiches from the tray to the inspector's plate. Inspector Rawlings offered him the bone and Buster's tail wagged from side to side so fast, his whole body moved as he grabbed the bone and trotted off to his basket by the fire, but he didn't settle, and changing his mind, he got up and walked over to the back door of the kitchen, where he stood waiting to be let out.

Faye got up from her chair, and as she opened the door for Buster, the sight of the green grass leading on to the meadow reminded her of Dollie's cottage and the gypsies that had been camped in the fields behind it. Her thoughts were interrupted by the sound of a horse's hooves trotting along the gravel track as someone rode down the side of the Station House and onto the bridal path.

"Inspector Rawlings, I've just remembered something I saw at Dollie's cottage. You wouldn't have known about it because of the fire," she said, sitting back down. "Before Greg came into the room, I found a map. It was on the floor in the dining room."

The inspector looked up from selecting another sandwich. "A map?"

"Yes. When I opened it, there was a line marked on the map."

"Oh," said the inspector, pausing, sandwich in hand.

"There was a line drawn on it from the woods at the Manor House, following the bridal path to a bridge. I can't remember what bridge it was," she said, a little annoyed for forgetting the detail.

"There's only one bridge there, Miss Lantern, that's Basset Woods and the bridge is Fawley Point. It's well known for the gypsies who do trading with horses and work, etc., along that canal." Still clutching his sandwich, the inspector jumped up. "I need to follow up on this new information about the map you've just mentioned."

Grabbing his coat from the back of the chair, he turned to Faye. "Once again, you have been most helpful."

He looked over to the chessboard and sighed. "Another time, then."

"Of course." She smiled, and the inspector left in a hurry for the station.

CHAPTER TWENTYTHREE

Lost Leads

A few weeks had passed, and the drama of the murders seemed to be subsiding, as Faye noticed it was no longer the first thing anyone spoke of when they saw her. She put on her coat and headed out of the Station House.

Gwen was rushed off her feet at the bakery, and her face lit up when she saw Faye walk in. "I haven't got time to chat," she said as she passed a brown paper bag full of tea cakes to one customer, whilst ringing change into the till with her other hand. "Tina, my part-time girl, isn't well and couldn't come in today." With that, she rushed off to get a loaf from the shelf behind her.

Faye could see the line of people building up as the queue flowed out of the shop and into the street. "Would you like a hand?" she asked.

Gwen didn't think twice as she said, "Grab the apron from the kitchen. You're a life saver!"

Faye saw that the shelves needed to be restocked and set about bringing the trays from the kitchen and filling up the racks with more sticky buns, cakes, and loaves of bread. By eleven o'clock, the rush had died down and Gwen had called the Saturday girl in to cover her. Taking off her apron, Faye followed Gwen to the back kitchen, where Gwen started making a pot of tea for them both. Faye noticed the plain white tiles across the kitchen were interrupted by colorful blue-and-white tiles dotted around the sink and walls, depicting horses walking along the canal towpath pulling barges. A black, cast-iron bakery oven, sprawled out across the center of the wall, was flanked by metal shelves with an assortment of round and long baking trays and loaf tins lined up in rows, sitting next to ceramic mixing bowls. Wooden spoons nestled together stood upright in a jug, next to a white canister with the word "flour" written in black across the front. Cast-iron pots and pans were dotted around on tops and on the floor, and an old wooden bakery table occupied the middle of the room with a collection of wooden rolling pins lying across it, still covered in flour from the morning's baking. Although a working kitchen, it had a quaint feel about it. They sat down next to the stove, and Faye breathed a sigh of relief.

"That was a lot of work!" she said, as Gwen opened the door of the stove and added some more logs.

"So, you won't be opening your own bakery any time soon, then." Gwen laughed.

"I don't think I could manage a bakery after today!" Faye replied, laughing with her.

Gwen sipped on her tea. "Although," she said hesitantly, "you know the Station House used to be the village tearooms."

Faye remembered Mrs. Field had mentioned it to her at the police station. Faye also remembered discovering a huge room and kitchen that had a separate double door to the side of the house, and it made sense now Gwen mentioned the tearooms.

"It would be nice to have a tearoom up and running again in the village," Gwen said, holding her cup in both hands, peering over the rim of the cup at Faye.

Faye stared at Gwen, puzzled. "You mean to say there isn't a tearoom here in the village . . . at all?"

"No. Not since the Station House closed its doors."

Faye's mind flitted back to the large room she had seen when she visited the Station House for the first time. She thought about her paintings and how it would make a great studio, as the big windows flooded the room with sunlight, right up to the beams on the ceiling and down the walls, creating a bright, airy room with a feeling of warmth about it.

"Maybe there's hope?" Gwen said with a glint in her eye.

Faye half smiled, staying silent, still deep in thought. It would be a new chapter in her life, a new start to put the murders behind her. Greg had still not been caught, but the inspector was following leads and she felt like it was time to put it all behind her. She turned to Gwen.

"Would you help me?"

Gwen looked puzzled. "Help you? How?"

"I think I'm going to open the Station House Tearoom again!"

Gwen let out a squeal of delight and jumped up from her chair and rushed over to hug Faye, as she always did when she was happy.

"That's so exciting! Of course, I'll help." And before the day was through, the whole village was talking about the news of the Station House Tearoom opening again.

CHAPTER TWENTYFOUR

The Tearoom

Faye had to forget the past and move forward, and she sat down, pen in hand. She wanted to get organized and made a list of all the things she needed to do to get the tearoom ready for the opening day. Gwen was at the forefront of the workforce, all of whom were villagers that had offered their help for free.

There was a buzz of excitement in the village, and Faye was in awe of the number of volunteers that had shown up. Gwen was telling people where to put tins of paint and brushes. Daniel had rolled up his sleeves and was moving tables with some of the men, out into the yard to keep them away from any paint splashing on them. Faye could see Mrs. Field with a neatly tied, white-and-purple head scarf wrapped around her head, putting on a matching apron, getting ready to start cleaning down the dressers. She pulled at the storage sheets covering the dressers, sending dust clouds ascending into the air. Rosemary and her mother came to collect the tablecloths and napkins ready to be laundered, and noticing Faye, Rosemary walked over to her hand in hand with Archie, who was about three years old.

"I just wanted to say thank you," she said, stepping forward to hug Faye.

Faye wished people wouldn't keep doing that and stood still, waiting for Rosemary to step back from her.

"You saved me, and now I have my—" She looked around before whispering, "Son back with me." As tears of happiness rolled down her cheeks, she added, "I can't thank you enough."

"You are most welcome," Faye said softly. "I'm so glad things worked out for you in the end."

At that moment, chaos broke out as a ladder fell, knocking a pot of green paint over, which spilled onto the floor.

"Don't worry," Faye called out. "I'll get some old towels." Saying goodbye to Rosemary and her mother, she walked through the back of the tearoom and into the yard outside. The sun was beaming down, and it felt good to feel the warmth of the rays on her face as she walked to the far end of her yard. A wave of happiness crept over her as she thought about the many new friends she had made and the exciting new adventure about to begin, as she opened the tearoom in a few days.

Turning the corner, she came across a weathered shed, hidden just out of sight of the yard, and unlatching the door, she stepped inside. She rummaged about until she found some old white sheets and towels in one of the large cupboards.

"There they are," she said aloud and bundled them up in her arms. She walked out, leaving the door open, as she could only just see above the bundle of sheets and towels in her arms. She would come back later to close it, she thought as she used her foot to open the door back into the tearoom.

The backyard fell silent behind her, the only noise coming from the shed door slowly closing as a hand pushed it shut. A hooded silhouette of a man stood in the shadows, before moving back out of sight.

***

As a few of the younger lads from the village brought the tables back into the tearoom from the yard, Daniel moved the last one into place.

"That's me done for today," he said, kissing Faye on the cheek as he put his coat on. "Jake's waiting outside for me. It's the office skittles night, and I want to be early and get on the winning team."

"How do you know which will be the wining team?" she asked, puzzled.

"Oh, that's easy," Daniel replied. "Whatever team the boss is on." Faye laughed as he added, "Don't wait up for me. These things are usually a drunken affair, and I'll stagger to Jake's house, as it's only a few doors down from the pub."

As Daniel ran out the door, Faye noticed the sky had turned gray and rain clouds loomed ominously above. She began to shut the tearoom door on the last few helpers that were leaving.

"We'll be back tomorrow," Gwen called out, waving as her pace quickened to avoid the downpour of rain just starting to fall.

The Station House fell silent once more, and all Faye wanted to do was relax into a warm bath, followed by a peaceful night's sleep. She finished locking up and went upstairs. She couldn't remember if she had locked the door to the yard earlier and stopped on the stairs. She looked at Buster, who was hot on her heels, ready to curl up on his cushion by her bed. *I'm sure I did,* she thought, remembering the door closing behind her as she brought the sheets and towels in. With the bath run, Faye relaxed back and smiled, gratefully recalling all the villagers and their help. After a long soak, she put on her nightgown and climbed into bed. Relaxed, she fell to sleep that night, unaware that the yard door had been left ajar after the last of the tables had been brought in, and she was not alone.

CHAPTER TWENTYTFIVE

Following the Trail

Faye rarely had nightmares anymore, but tonight, she awoke abruptly. Buster was grumbling under his breath, before breaking into a low, deep bark.

"Buster. What is it?" Faye opened her eyes. The moonlight lit up her bedroom, and there, at the end of her bed, stood a hooded figure. Paralyzed by fear, she sat motionless as he stepped forward, the moonlight catching his face.

"Greg!" she gasped, just before she felt a sharp blow to her head.

***

Daniel arrived back at the Station House early the next morning feeling a little worse for wear. He called out to Faye, and not hearing a reply, thought she was still sleeping. It had been a long day yesterday, and today would be no exception, he thought. Walking into the kitchen, he realized something wasn't quite right. It suddenly dawned on him that Buster was not there to greet him as he usually did.

"Buster," he called out. "Buster? Where are you?"

He could hear a faint whimpering sound coming from somewhere but couldn't quite place it.

An anxious feeling came over him as he headed to the bottom of the stairs.

"Auntie Faye?" he called again.

Still no reply.

"Buster. Where are you, boy?" he called up and heard a scratching sound, followed by the faint bark of Buster coming from upstairs. "Auntie Faye?" Climbing to the top of the stairs, he knocked on her bedroom door.

Buster started barking, and Daniel cautiously opened the door. Buster rushed out, spinning in circles, wagging his tail and body in his excitement to see Daniel, who bent down to greet him.

"Hey there, Buster," he said, trying to hold Buster away from furiously licking his face. He looked over to see Faye's bed was empty. He walked over and placed his hand on the sheets. They were stone cold. Faye had not slept there. He stood there for a moment, puzzled, trying to think where Faye could be. He went back downstairs, followed by Buster, and picked up the telephone.

Gwen was getting ready to leave to start the day at the Station House when she answered the telephone to Daniel.

"What do you mean, Faye's missing?" she said back to Daniel when he discovered Gwen didn't know where Faye was either.

"She hasn't slept in her bed. She's nowhere to be found."

"I'm on my way over now," she said, before hanging up the receiver, and left immediately for the Station House.

Daniel had already been on the telephone to Inspector Rawlings, who arrived with another officer at the same time as Gwen. Inspector Rawlings went into Faye's bedroom and looked around. He then proceeded to walk through every room in the house, every now and then stopping to take a closer look before walking out into the backyard. There had been no sign of forced entry, and his eyes scoured the ground, looking for footprints and any other clues. He stopped suddenly as his eye caught sight of a white cigarette butt, lying on the floor outside the door. He took out a white handkerchief from his top pocket and carefully picked up the cigarette butt. Turning the handkerchief over to look at it, his heart sank as he recognized the brand, Marlboro—it was the same brand they had found at Dorothy Mahoney's cottage, and the same brand of cigarette that Greg Bulmer smoked.

Inspector Rawlings went back through the Station House and into the front of the tearoom, where Gwen and the other villagers were gathering, ready for another day of work in preparation for the opening. Daniel was stood with Buster by the window, watching Inspector Rawlings as he walked in, searching for a clue in his face that he might have found something. The inspector held the rolled-up handkerchief out to the other police officer.

"See this gets back to the station."

Buster suddenly started barking, pulling on his lead.

"Buster, what's got into you?" Daniel said, pulling him back. "This isn't like you." But Buster kept jumping around frantically, pulling him forward again.

Inspector Rawlings noticed it was out of character for Buster, too. "I think he's trying to tell us something."

Buster was pulling again, harder now, making Daniel stumble forward.

"Let him lead you to what's bothering him," the inspector called out, and Daniel tightened his grip on Buster's lead as he was half-walked and half-dragged by Buster, who was jumping forward with his two front paws in the air, pulling on his collar to get moving.

Daniel was now running behind as Buster had his nose to the ground, sniffing, veering left and right, until he suddenly let out a bark and took off. Daniel lurched forward, hanging on to Buster's lead for dear life.

Inspector Rawlings, who was running close behind with his coattails flying, shouted to Daniel, "I think he's picked up a scent."

Gwen called out, "Wait! I'm coming too!" as she rushed to follow Inspector Rawlings as he disappeared into the woodland.

Buster suddenly stopped by a large fallen oak tree lying across the path and started barking and whining.

"What have you found, boy?" the inspector asked, out of breath as he reached Buster. He looked down to see a Marlboro cigarette butt lying on the floor. "Good lad," the inspector said, praising Buster.

But Buster hadn't finished, as he followed the scent up and over the fallen tree to a thicket and stopped. The inspector could see a torn piece of floral material dangling from one of the sharp thicket barbs. He looked at Daniel, who nodded in silent confirmation it was from Faye's nightgown.

Hearing a lot of noise coming from the path behind him, the inspector turned to see Gwen appear with all the villagers from the teahouse following close behind her.

"What's happened?" she screamed hysterically. "Have you found Faye?"

"No. Calm down, Gwen," he said sternly. "We don't need any hysterics from you or anyone else!"

Clearing his throat, he addressed Gwen and the villagers, who were all assembled. "I think I know where Buster is leading us, and it's not safe. I understand you want to help, but you are impeding the investigation. The best thing you can do right now is to go home."

As some of them complained, he stared at Gwen expectantly, waiting for her to speak up. She realized what he was doing and turned to everyone.

"Tom—the inspector is right. It's not safe, and we may be trampling and ruining evidence that might help to find Faye. Let's go back and do what we came here to do, help Faye get the tearoom ready to open again. We can wait for news about her from there."

George, who had also come along to help, recognized that they were heading for Fawley Point Bridge and was aware of the possible dangers of arriving like a mob at the bridge. He stepped forward next to Gwen.

"I agree with the inspector. It looks like we're headed to Fawley Point Bridge, and it's no place for any of us to be."

Inspector Rawlings breathed a sigh of relief as his police officers came into view, passing the villagers, who were heading back.

"Right, men. Stay alert and don't do anything without my say so." And with that, they set off behind Buster, who was again dragging Daniel further into the woods toward Fawley Point Bridge.

CHAPTER TWENTYTSIX

Fawley Point Bridge

Coming to, Faye could feel her face was swollen and winced with pain as she tried to open her eyes to look around. A blackened, grey carpet rolled out along the middle of a walkway was covered in muddy footprints, and stained seating cushions, which she could see were once a shade of blue, sat squarely on either side on top of wooden seating. There was a damp smell in the air around her, and she could feel the rope cutting into her wrists as she put her hands down, pushing herself up onto her knees. She could see the long windows that stretched to either side of her. She instantly recognized the barge that had been traveling the canal a few days ago whilst she was feeding the ducks. Her throat was dry, and she moved the cloth that was around her mouth with her jaw, trying to loosen it before pulling it free. She could hear shouting and looked through the window to see two men arguing outside. She watched a heavy-set man in a white shirt and braces throw the first punch on a smaller man who instantly went back at him, losing his cap as he went fists flying in a rage. In the distance, she saw another man running forward as the two men wrestled to the ground. He grabbed one man, pulling him back by his shirt, and stepped in between them, separating them as they scrambled to their feet.

Holding each one back with his hands on their chests, he shouted at the smaller one of them, "She can't stay on the barge. Go get her."

The larger man started swearing at him, arguing with him, as the other man picked up his cap, and dusting it off, started walking toward her. Faye's heart started racing as she watched him put on his cap and jump onto the barge. The man stood in front of her, breathing heavily. Faye didn't recognize him and flinched as he moved toward her. Her stomach turned as she smelled a mixture of sweat and alcohol when he bent down to pull her up by the arms.

"Where are you taking me?" she screamed.

"Away from here!" he replied, pushing her forward.

As they stepped up on deck, Faye started to shiver. The wind had picked up, and she only had her nightgown on. Rain started to fall as she stumbled barefoot off the barge and onto the grass verge, and her heart stopped when she saw Greg's face come into view. He had blood running down his face and onto his white shirt. Faye realized he had been the other man in the fight, dressed as a traveler. She stumbled as the man shoved his hand into her back, pushing her toward Greg.

"We don't want no coppers snooping round 'ere 'cause of her," he snarled menacingly.

Faye could feel her body start to tremble, and as she stood terrified, facing Greg, she thought she heard the faint sound of Buster's bark. She looked over into the woods and saw a man running through the trees, calling out to the two travelers.

"Move it!" he called out frantically. "Now!" he shouted even louder at them when he realized they were still standing there. The two men took flight, following him down the canal path at lightning speed, and rounding the bend, they disappeared out of sight.

Greg lurched forward, grabbing Faye by the throat. She could see the rage in his eyes as he squeezed his hand tighter. She fell back, her tied hands trying desperately to pull his arm down and away from her throat. Gasping for air, she watched as his face twisted and snarled, drawing closer to hers.

"I wanted you to suffer, but I'm going to make you pay instead. You'll never testify against me." He pushed against her throat even harder, and Faye started to feel lightheaded. She thought she heard Buster's bark again, and that was her last thought before everything went black.

CHAPTER TWENTYSEVEN

Life and Death

Faye could hear voices. Not clearly at first, but the familiar feel of Buster smothering her with kisses, licking her face over and over, brought her round, until she could hear someone saying, "Miss Lantern?"

She opened her eyes to see Inspector Rawlings and Daniel standing over her, looking down at her with worried expressions on their faces.

"Thank the Lord," Daniel said, bending down to kneel on the grass where she was lying. "I thought you were a goner for sure!"

"Thank you for that observation, Daniel," Inspector Rawlings interrupted, "but I think that's enough of that talk."

He turned to the police officer standing next to him and said, "Pemberley, go and find a horse and cart to get Miss Lantern up to the village, and bring a car there to meet us."

Turning back to Faye, he said, "We'll be taking you to the hospital."

Faye was too weak to answer, and within minutes, she found herself lying in the back of the cart, feeling every bump along the track until they reached the village.

Inspector Rawlings immediately jumped into action. Waving his arms about, he shouted out, “Keep back! Give us some room,” keeping everyone at bay.

Faye heard the gasps as they carried her off the cart and into the waiting police car. Closing her eyes, she realized she’d become the focus of the village gossip once more.

CHAPTER TWENTYEIGHT

Hidden Secrets

Faye could hear a nurse speaking with the doctor, who turned, noticing Faye was stirring. As her eyes adjusted to the light, he came into view. She could see he was standing at the end of the bed, clipboard in hand, with a broad smile across his face. He placed a pen in the top pocket of his white coat and walked over to her.

"How are you feeling after your little adventure, Faye?" he asked.

Faye whispered back in a hoarse voice, "Better now. Thank you."

"Good. Well, you'll be pleased to know you haven't sustained any life-threatening injuries. You have some bruising and swelling to the trachea . . . your throat. And some minor cuts and bruises, but overall, I think you came off quite well, all things considered. If you rest and don't talk too much, I see no reason why you can't go home in a day or two, once the swelling in your throat has gone down."

Faye nodded her appreciation as she whispered, "Thank you," and closed her eyes again. She heard the doctor walk outside, and after a brief conversation, he returned with Inspector Rawlings.

"Just a few minutes. She really needs to rest," the doctor instructed him and left them alone.

Faye could see the concerned look on Inspector Rawlings's face as he said, "Good to see you are awake, Miss Lantern. How are you feeling?"

Slowly managing to sit upright in the bed, Faye replied in little more than a whisper, "My throat is a little sore, but okay."

He nodded as he sat down in the chair next to her bed. "The doctor says you should make a good recovery." He paused for a moment before continuing, "I just stopped by to let you know we have Greg Bulmer in custody."

Faye's eyes closed briefly in relief as she heard the news.

"He won't be bothering you again. I just thought you would want to know."

"Thank you, Inspector, that is a great comfort to hear." Gathering her breath again, she asked, "How did you find me?"

She saw a broad smile spread across his face as he replied, "All I can say is you have a very good tracker dog in Buster. He led us straight to the bridge. He's a handy dog to have around when you're in a tight spot. We saw the two travelers running down the towpath as Buster led us to you, at the canal." His tone grew serious. "That's when I saw Greg with his hand at your throat. He dropped you and ran, but I had him in my sights. He wasn't getting away. That's where a good rugby tackle comes in handy," he said matter-of-factly.

Faye leaned her head back on the pillow as the inspector added, "All in all, it's been quite an eventful few days." He stood up from the chair, noticing Faye was getting tired. "You'll need to testify at the trial . . . when you're feeling better."

"Yes. Of course."

"I'll be off, then, Miss Lantern, and let you get some rest." He strode to the door and stopped, turning back to look at Faye. "Gwen tells me you're going to reopen the tearoom at the Station House?"

"That was the plan," Faye whispered. "But the decorating will have to wait until I'm recovered."

"You don't need to worry yourself about that. I believe it's all going on full steam ahead. The villagers are rallying round, hard at work trying to get as much done before your return as they can. They will do you proud," he said, and tipping his hat to her, left Faye to her thoughts.

After all she had been through, she still felt happy to be part of the village. She thought of Gwen and George and all the other people who were selflessly helping her to reopen the tearoom, and she smiled as an inner sense of peace came over her. Her mind wandered to the opening day of the tearoom. It seemed so simple, just like moving house, as long as she was organized, but then her mind took her to the murders as she'd moved into the Station House, and the terror she had endured at the hands of Greg Bulmer. Fear stirred in her, and she wondered whether reopening the tearoom would be as simple as she hoped for, or whether it would open the door to more trouble. Before she closed her eyes again, there was a swift knock at the door.

"I've got to be quick!" Gwen said, poking her head around the door before stepping in and hastily walking across the room, carrying a small wicker basket over her arm. "I talked my way past the nurse, but she really didn't want you to have any more visitors, so I told her I would be really quick."

Faye could see a huge smile across Gwen's face as she reached the bed, and Faye winced, ready for her to lean in and hug her, but was grateful when instead, Gwen stepped back.

"Oh, you poor thing," she said, concerned, as she saw Faye's swollen face.

"It's not as bad as it looks," Faye rasped.

"Oh, your throat sounds so sore, and that's a nice shiner you've got there! I can't believe this has happened to you. I'm so sorry."

She reached into the basket she was carrying and started pulling out grapes and apples and little fondant cakes. "Just in case you get hungry in the night," she said and started hiding them in Faye's bedside cupboard.

"Thank you. I'm pleased you're here," Faye said, her voice still hoarse as she spoke.

"What are friends for if we can't support each other? Talking of which, I have some news for you." Gwen's happy demeanor suddenly changed, and Faye guessed that it wasn't good news. "I was going to wait until you came out of hospital to tell you, but I bumped into Tom . . . Inspector Rawlings as I came in, and he said you could be out in a day or two, and I wanted to let you know first."

Faye started to feel a knot in her stomach as she waited for Gwen to tell her the bad news.

"I wanted to let you know that one of the lads helping with the decorating knocked a ladder over and it fell, well, hit really, the teahouse wall and went through it."

"Oh, is that all?" Faye said, relieved.

"Well, not quite," Gwen said anxiously. "When he pulled the ladder out, it left a gaping hole, and . . ." She paused, before blurting out, "There was a dead body in there!"

Faye's eyes widened in disbelief and a searing pain went through her swollen eye, making her recoil back into the pillow.

She could see panic on Gwen's face as she put her hands to her mouth and gasped, "I shouldn't have told you yet. I'm so sorry."

"Really, it's okay," Faye said, trying to reassure her.

"When I said dead body, I meant a skeleton. A full skeleton . . . of a man, they think, so he has been dead for quite a while," Gwen added, trying her best to make it sound better. "They are waiting for the inspector to get there now, and I just wanted to tell you first, you know, before any tongues start wagging."

Faye was stunned into silence, trying to take it all in. "Do they have any idea who it is?"

Gwen shrugged. "Only that it's most likely a man, because of its height and size." She leaned in toward Faye. "Funny thing is," she whispered, "old Mrs. Penny, who you brought the Station House from, well, her husband went missing a few years ago, and no one knows what happened to him. I reckon something funny must have gone on there, and I bet a pound to a penny that it will be Mr. Penny's pile of bones tucked away in that wall!"

The door opened, and Faye could see the nurse walk in and fix her gaze on Gwen. Looking at her watch and then back to Gwen, she said abruptly, "Visiting time is over!"

"I'll pop by tomorrow, then," Gwen said sheepishly and slunk past the nurse and out the door.

"Yes, tomorrow. Thank you for—" Faye didn't finish the sentence, as she didn't want the nurse to know about the basket of goodies Gwen had stashed in her bedside cupboard—just in case she got hungry in the night. As the nurse shut the door behind herself, Faye closed her eyes, glad to have peace again. Her mind drifted to the day Mr. Grimmer had shown her around the Old Station House. He'd mentioned that Mrs. Penny was frail and had gone into a retirement home, and Faye was sure she couldn't have had anything to do with the skeleton in the wall.

She drifted off into a fitful sleep, knowing another murder investigation was about to take place, and she and her tearoom were at the heart of it all . . .

We Value Your Opinion and Would Love

to Hear From you

What did you think of Faye Lantern and the Search for the Village Murderer?

First of all, thank you for purchasing my book, ***Faye Lantern and the Search for the Village murderer****. I know you could have picked any number of books to read, but you picked this book and for that I am extremely grateful.*

I hope that it added value and quality to your everyday life. If so, it would be really nice if you could share this book with your friends and family by posting to Facebook and Twitter.

If you enjoyed this book and found some benefit in reading this, I'd like to hear from you and hope that you could take some time to post a review on Amazon. Your feedback and support will help this author to greatly improve her writing craft for future projects and make this book even better.

You can follow this link now.

I want you, the reader, to know that your review is very important and so, if you'd like to ***leave a review****, all you have to do is just* ***scan the barcode below****, and away you go. I wish you all the best in your future success!*

Discover more from

Penny Townsend

Visit: www.pennytownsend.com for:

New Book Announcements

~

Book Extracts

~

You can sign up to Penny's newsletter to get updates

On her books and gain access to exclusive offers – scan the QR code below:

Milton Keynes UK
Ingram Content Group UK Ltd.
UKHW030700170824
447045UK00001B/22